H-Blocc

– Ariel Acosta

*H-BLOCC
- Ariel Acosta
"King & Queen Publishing"
Copyright © 2021
ISBN:*

*Instagram Page: @king.queenpublishing
FaceBook Page: @kingandqueenpublishing
Website: https://www.kingandqueenpublishing.org/
Email: info@kingandqueenpublishing.org
Cashapp: $kingqueenpublishing*

Dedication

First and foremost, I would like to dedicate this book to God, for all the blessings he has blessed me with.

I also dedicate this book to my son Ivan, my daughter Hailey and to their mother Aisha; for blessing me with two wonderful kids.

To all my Harlems that's standing tall no matter what their circumstances are; to my brothers – Lil Shrico, Jay Three, Boobie; my sisters – Carina, Julissa and Jerelyn: I love y'all with all my heart, I do this for y'all!

I also want to dedicate this book to all my homies: Danny, J-Rocc, Lefty, Dom Rolla, AR Rolla, Fatboii Rolla, Stew Rolla, Reddot Rolla and Tsunami. I thank all y'all niggas for keeping it 100% no matter what! They don't make 'em like y'all anymore. I love y'all niggas! You know the vibes; what don't break us can only make us stronger!

This book is also dedicated to my fallen soldiers 'OG Premo' and 'Crandon Loco'; I love and miss y'all niggas dearly! Just know that we down here makin sure y'all names are never forgotten! Y'all would always live through my music and my books.

Last but not least, to my Big Crody: King Thomas for believing in me and my talents as an author!

#LEGENDARYSHIT!
#TOP30SHIT!
#380BABIES
#KING&QUEENPUBLISHING
TAKING OVER THE GAME!

Acknowledgment

Once again I would love to thank the man above, for all the blessings and everythin He has done and continues to do for me and my family; now that I got that out of the way, I would like to give a shout out to all my family and friends.

Big shout out to my Hughes niggas! Japan, Spade, Trey Pizzy and the whole ROCC GANG! To my loc – Miggz and the whole 1-9-9: Silly, Dirt, Purp, Gutta and Lou. Stratford, I see y'all! "83" BIZ, P-Gutta, Bobby, Rowdy, Meeshie, Cueno and my whole 'GS9' family!

To my BIG MONEY NIGGAS: Tyliek (a.k.a) 'Trey Shot Balla, Tick Tick, Will and Ziico Niiko. You know I can't forget about my BRONX NIGGAS – Keiffy Balla, 'BSV' Mills, Mel, Fatal Balla. My 'CT – NJ – LI' niggas: BG from Brookdale Newark, Fresh, Bum Jew, Ty-Ty, Nyce, Mainey-O, Blue, 'Tampa' Cuzzy, L. Farmer and my nigga R.Murphy #067 (a.k.a) Nas.

To my locsta – Chewy Da Grap3! SUGARHILL, we're in the building! Oh, before I forget my Y-O Niggas – Fatal Brim, Lingo Loc and 'Murder Ville' Kritter.

There're too many names to mention, but y'all know who you are: I love y'all. If I forgot any name, it wasn't intentional and I promise to get y'all on the next one!

"HHHHHHHHHH-BLLLLOOOOOOCCCCCCCCC!!!"

Y'all niggas better fasten y'all seat belts! KING & QUEEN PUBLISHING IS COMING TO TAKE OVER THE GAME!

Prologue
"Hoodie season"

"Yo Goldo, spin the blocc one more time" Lil Rico said from the back seat. He was becoming frustrated, as the thought of them leaving without getting what they had come for, invaded his thoughts.

Goldo did as he was told and drove the 1995 Honda Civic around the block once more. Though they didn't see the person they had been looking for, they were about ready to call it a night; but at the last minute, the breakthrough they all had been looking for finally presented itself.

"Oh shit! There goes the nigga right there!" Lil Rico shouted spotting the target standing in front of the Six Train Station on 138 St., Brook Avenue. *"Where? where?"* True Blue asked as he also scanned through the block trying to locate their target.

A smile spread across True Blue's face as the thought of the $60,000.00 that they were minutes away from getting ran through his mind. *"Right there! Standing on the corner, talking to the Mexican nigga!"* Lil Rico exclaimed. *"Turn to the corner and park after a few cars,"* he then added.

Goldo did as he was told and made the left turn onto Brook Avenue, just like Lil Rico had instructed. The target and his friend finally parted ways, with his friend disappearing into the train station. The target made his way towards his parked car.

5

Shortly after Goldo had parked the car, True Blue and Lil Rico jumped out of the car with one thing in mind; secure the bag! By the time they reached the target's car, he had already gotten into it.

Lucky they got there when they did; because the Honda Civic would have never been able to keep up with the speed of the almost $200,000.00 worth car if he had jumped on the highway. *"Pssshhh! Vroooomm!!"* was all that was heard as the spaceship-looking car came to life making True Blue and Lil Rico stop in their track for a second. It was just that, a second.

Before the loan shark knew what was taking place, True Blue had already snatched the car door open while Lil Rico aimed the .38 revolver at his head, all in one motion. *"Dame el maletin!"* True Blue said in Spanish, demanding the black messenger bag that the loan shark carried around his neck.

It didn't take long for the target to figure-out what was going on. As he spotted the black revolver that was being held to his face, his heart started beating faster in his chest. Without a second thought, he removed the messenger bag from around his neck and threw it at True Blue.

The loan shark was parked in a secluded area, which made the robbery that was taking place much easier. *"Please no kill! Please no me mate."* The target begged for his life. Reaching to his pockets, he then handed True Blue two thick bundles of cash as well as the Cuban link bracelet that he wore around his wrist.

Immediately the money and the bracelet were secured in his pockets, True Blue then reached out to remove the finger thick matching Cuban link chain from his neck as well. Satisfied with their work, True Blue and Lil Rico then made their exit; but not before removing the car keys from the ignition as well.

Chapter One

True Blue sat in the (GRVC) better known as the beacon and couldn't help but to ask himself; *"How the fuck did I end up back in this shit?"*

The last time he was housed in the beacon, he had promised himself to do everything in his power to never step foot back into this shit hole; but here was, after doing three and a half years in State Prison; and only three months of being home, he was back on a parole violation.

True Blue was also being held on a $10,000.00 bail for a pending robbery case that he had been fighting for the past two years. The parole violation was the least of his worries, because he only had 3 more months until his out date; but the thought of having to do any time for the pending robbery case was weighing heavy on his mind.

True Blue was relaxing on top of one of the tables in the dayroom room enjoying a bag of the Doritos with a Slim Jim as he watch the TV He normally didn't like watching the stupid box, but being that they were playing the latest music videos he was all for it; not trying to miss it.

Some of the other inmate stood by the TV watching the videos as well. The latest music video for the New York rapper 'Casanova' hit single 'Don't Run' had just come on the TV as all the inmates started standing by the TV. It was getting harder for True Blue to watch the video.

"*Ayo, Touch, watch out cuhz, a nigga can't even see the TV!*" True Blue yelled, trying to get his homeboys attention. Being that the TV was on full blast on top of the inmates talking amongst each other, Touch wasn't able to hear True Blue.

"*Yo Touch, move the fucc out the way loc!*" True Blue repeated, with a little more base in his voice. This time Touch heard him loud and clear and turned around to face him. "*Nigga, if yuh tryin to watch this shit so bad, then stand the fucc up just like we doin!*" Touch shot back, with too much hostility for True Blue's liking.

"*Nigga, I don't have to stand for shit! Nigga move out my way foh, yuh movin like yuh don't already know my body!*" True Blue retorted. By now he was standing on top of the table, ready to take it where ever Touch was trying to take it. True Blue was a hot head fellow and was always ready for some wreck.

"*Fucc all that! I don't want to talk, yuh know watssup nigga!*" True Blue added as he stepped off the table and made his way over to the blind spot at the end of the tier. The blind spot was where anybody could go, if and when they wanted to get their shit off without the Police being able to spot them.

Although True Blue ain't say much, Touch knew that he was calling him out. Shit, the whole unit did; that was an unspoken call out. Three whole minutes had passed and Touch was moving like he ain't seen True Blue standing back there waiting on him.

"Bitch ass nigga!" True Blue said to himself as he walked away from the blind spot in the direction of his cell. Once in his cell, he made his way over to the small table that rested at the back of the small cell and picked up his phone Book.

After the confrontation with Touch, he decided to give his little Boo Christal a call to see if she was still coming to see him on Saturday. Before he was able to walk back out the cell, his main man Meeshie had just walked in the cell. The name sound familiar because you heard his name on Bobby Shmurda's hit single 'Hot Nigga.'

Standing at 5 feet 8, about 170lbs with corn rows to the back of his neck; a brown skin with about 5 inches cut on the side of his left cheek from a previous bid in Up North State prison. *"wat the fucc happen with yuh n Touch cuhz?"* Meeshie asked, catching True Blue by surprise. Meeshie was on a visit when the whole thing with Touch went down.

"*That shit ain't bout nothin cuhz, that nigga don't want no smoke.*" True Blue shot back, brushing the whole thing off. "*Nigga if yuh want to go over there n flip that nigga, we can go left now cuhz!*" Meeshie retorted, ready to put in some work, like always.

See, if True Blue wanted to jump Touch; that would have been an easy thing to do. But, that wasn't what he wanted to do. He loved himself in a one on one, any day, with anybody. "*Nah loco fucc that nigga.*" True Blue retorted. "*How was ya visit tho?*" he then asked Meeshie changing the subject.

"*That shit was Litisha Crody! Shawty was down there lookin like a snacc; had a nigga ready to tear her clothes off!*" Meeshie shot back and they both shared a laugh. "*She said that she comin bacc up here on Saturday,*" he added.

"*Oh word! Shit, we might be down there together; Christal said she might be pullin up on Saturday as well.*" True Blue said. "*I'm about to call her now and see watssup.*" He continued.

"*Aight bet, say that then! I'm about to go in my cell n change out this monkey suit*" Meeshie said, making his way out of True Blue's cell. After, True Blue grabbed his phone Book off his desk and exited the cell on his way to give his little Boo a call.

Ever since the incident with True Blue took place; Touch decided to play his cell closed; not because he was scared, but because he rather have his back against the wall just in case anything jumped off. Especially after seeing Meeshie get back from his visit and go straight into True Blue's cell.

Touch knew that nothing good could have come out of the two of them. Touch was a Crip and was also from the Bronx. He stood 6 feet 1, 180 lbs, dark as the color of charcoal, with a few tattoos covering his body.

Touch was far from a scared nigga, but he knew that he ain't having any win with True Blue; especially not with all his homies in the same unit as they were. After Touch had calmed down, he knew that he was wrong for the way that he had come at True Blue.

Therefore, Touch wanted to fix it before things went any further. Seeing Meeshie finally exit True Blue's cell not too long after he spotted True Blue exit the cell as well; and make his way over towards the phones

"Ayo! True Blue! When yuh get the chance, I need to holla at yuh cuhz" Touch yelled, getting True Blue's attention. *"Not right now cuhz, it can wait till yuh get off the jack,"* he added, seeing that True Blue was about to make his

12

way over. True Blue nodded his head and focused his attention back on the phone.

Chapter Two

After Meeshie walked out of True Blue's cell, he made his way over to his cell which was right next to Touch's cell. Meeshie was in cell 7 and Touch in cell 6. Meeshie walked right past Touch and went into his cell without saying a word to him.

Once in his cell, he started Removing the tan two piece jump suit that they had the inmates wearing every time that they left their unit; only leaving the white t-shirt he had on under it. He couldn't believe how True Blue decided to let Touch slide just like that.

Meeshie figured that Touch was lucky because the old True Blue would have been ran his mouth; no questions asked. As he traded his tans for his grey sweat pants, Meeshie couldn't help but to think about the time he had spent with Shanice on their visit. She was looking real sexy and he couldn't wait to see her again that Saturday.

Once he put on his sweats, he hopped on his feet and threw on his all black Puma GV specials. Walking over to his food bucket, he reached inside of it and took out everything he needed to make himself a nice cup of coffee. Afterwards, he walked out of his cell and made his way over to the hot pot.

On his way towards the hot pot, Meeshie heard his man Jada yelling and slamming the cards on the table as he played a game of spades. *"He must be winnin."* Meeshie thought to himself as he let the hot water pour into his cup from the spigot.

True Blue and Meeshie had met awhile back, while both serving State time Up North where Crippin wasn't easy, but it sure was fun. Once they met, they had cliqued on the spot; real recognizing real.

When they both returned home from serving their State time, Meeshie and True Blue linked up in the streets and continued to build a bond that stretched way past the jail walls. When Meeshie finished getting his water for his cup of coffee, he made his way over towards the tables, but not before looking over towards the phones.

"Damn that nigga loves them phones," he thought to himself, spotting True Blue still on the phone. Taking a seat on the table, Meeshie sipped out of his cup of mud while watching the re-runs of the music videos they had been playing all morning.

"This nigga needs to hurry up off that phone, a nigga trynna get his mind right," Meeshie said to himself, looking over towards the phones once again. While sitting on the table, he felt like someone was looking at him; turning

around, he spotted Touch turning his face away, as if he wasn't just burning a hole on his back.

Meeshie brushed it off with a laugh. *"Only if this bitch knew that niggas wasn't even worryin about him,"* he thought. If it was up to Meeshie, he would have flipped on Touch; but his main man said it wasn't about nothing, so he decided to leave Touch alone for now.

Without him knowing, Touch was walking on thin ice; and any little movement would have him falling into a hole that would be way too hard for him to get out off.

Chapter Three

"Good afternoon sexy!" True Blue said into the receiver when Christal answered her phone. *"Oh yeah! Hey handsome!"* Christal replied in the sexiest voice she could muster. *"Nothing here, missin ya sexy ass."* True Blue said coolly. *"Oh really? Why that sound like yuh over here tryin to game me?"* Christal quickly said.

"Come on now ma, yuh know I have no reason to be gamin yuh. A nigga do miss yuh, n I can't wait till I see yuh this weekend; to hug and kiss yuh while I grab a handful of that big juicy sexy ass of yours." True Blue assured her.

Christal was a bad Dominican and black beauty. Thick in all the right places, at 5 feet 5, she had enough ass to go around and still have enough left for herself. She resembles the actress Megan Good.

"Mmm, oh really?" Christal asked playing alone. *"Ohh yeah, reallllyyy."* True Blue shot back, dragging the word "really" for emphasis. *"Question sexy, are yuh still comin up here on Saturday?"* he then asked her. *"Of course I am Boo, I wouldn't miss it or want it any other way!"* Christal responded. *"Oh, Okay copy that, Boo"* True Blue responded.

True Blue and Christal went on to have a good conversation for the remainder of the call. When the phone finally beeped, they said their goodbyes with hopes of seeing one another the upcoming Saturday. *"Okay sexy, hope yuh continue to have a good one."* True Blue was able to say before the phone call was disconnected.

After ending the call with Christal, True Blue made his way over to where Touch was sitting to see what was it that he wanted to holla at him about. *"Ayo Touch, wats crackin cuhz, talk to me,"* True Blue said as soon as he reached the table where Touch was sitting at playing a game of casino.

"Nah, loc, I just wanted to let yuh know that a nigga ain't mean to come at yuh the way I did earlier. A nigga had gotten a bad phone call n just snapped loc," Touch said, lying through his teeth. The truth was that he wasn't trying to end up getting jumped by True Blue and his men.

"Man that shit ain't about nothin loco. A nigga ain't even on that shit no more fr fr" True Blue shot back, brushing the whole thing off like it was nothing. *"So, we good then loco?"* Touch asked, trying to assure his safety. *"Yeah cuhz, we gucci great!"* True Blue replied, extending his hand out to give Touch some dap.

True Blue made his way over to where Meeshie was sitting patiently waiting for his return. *"Nigga yuh tryin to watch this lame ass videos or yuh tryin to go get ya mind*

18

right?" True Blue asked, already knowing the answer to his question. Like him, Meeshie was also a hot head.

"Cuhz yuh already know my cody! I was waitin on ya lovey dovey ass to get of that fuckin phone." Meeshie shot back as he got up off the table. *"So, let's go then nigga."* True Blue retorted and then made his way over to the blind spot also known as the smoking section. Meeshie and KD followed close behind.

True Blue, Meeshie and KD sat on the floor while passing the three blunts that they had in rotation to one another. After smoking the first three blunts, KD decided to roll up another one, since it was almost count time. Once the last blunt was done, the trio made their way back down stairs and into the dayroom.

"Ayo, I'ma holla at ya niggas on the locc out; I'm about to go make me somethin to eat rite quicc cuhz." True Blue said, walking off in the direction of his cell. *"Wat yuh makin cuhz?"* Meeshie asked, before True Blue was completely in his cell; turning around he said *"Nothin too crazy cuhz, just an eggroll loco."*

Twenty minutes later, all the inmates had to return back to their cells and get ready for the four o-clock count. During the hour lock down, True Blue and Meeshie were in their cells doing the 550s, which consisted of ten sets of ten

19

all the way down to one; along with 200 burpies, 200 squats and 300 dips.

Chapter Four

Dread looked at the clock on the wall and it read 10:45pm. He couldn't wait until 11.00pm when his shift will finally be over. Dread had been at work for the past eight hour and couldn't wait to get back to his unit. He was the "S.P.A" in the special housing unit. Although the job had its perks, Dread hated the fact that he had to baby sit a grown ass man.

A few days prior, Dread had given his man Snoop $300 for him to burst a move for him. Three days past since then and snoop still haven't come back with his drugs nor money. Every time that Dread tried to confront him, Snoop always gave him the run around; and Dread was tired of all the games with his money.

Dread's gut feeling was telling him that something was off. Following his gut feeling, he had sent someone to holla at his man "Jay" for him to see if he had received the $300 dollars that he had sent him three days ago. Today, the word had gotten back to him from his man "Jay" that he never received nothing of Dread's.

"This nigga Snoop must think this shit a game," Dread thought to himself as he glanced at the clock one more time.*"Pearson! Get ya things ready! The escort is comin to get yuh!"* The officer shouted from inside of the bubble. Dread gathered all his belongings and prepared to leave.

21

Not too long after the escort had arrived and Dread walked out of the 'SHU' on his way back to his unit; being that it was almost midnight, he knew that he would have to wait till the next day to confront Snoop. When Dread got back to the unit, he noticed that all the lights in the cells were off, meaning one thing – everyone was already asleep.

When Dread arrived in the confinement of his cell, he took off the tan two piece; and then put on a pair of basketball shorts. Once comfortable he rolled himself a stick of weed and sparked it.

After he finished getting his mind right, he reached over to the top of his food bucket and grabbed the Book he had been reading called, 'Like Father, Like Son' by the author, A. A. Costa. After reading a few chapters, Dread felt his eyes getting heavy on him. Closing the Book, he placed it back on top of his food bucket. Not too long after, Dread was out for the count.

- - -

– The Next Day –

Dread woke up the next morning at 9.00am with one thing on his mind; to get to the bottom of Snoop's shenanigan. Rollin out of his bunk, Dread walked over to the small sink and began to brush his teeth and wash his face.

Once his hygiene was taken care of, Dread began to put on his all black Puma 'Roma'. Walking over to the door he looked out of the small cell window trying to see if he could spot Snoop; but to his luck he, didn't, which only meant one thing – Snoop was still in his cell.

"BOOM! BOOM!! BOOM!!!" Dread banged on his cell door window trying to get the attention of the CO-O on duty; he finally got her attention as she walked over to his cell door and locked him out. *"Good morning Ms. Rodriguez,"* Dread said to the CO-O as he walked out of his cell. *"Good morning Pearson,"* she responded, with a smile on her face as she turned around and walked off.

Dread couldn't help but to stare at her basketball shaped ass. Ms. Rodriguez was this sexy Dominican beauty, standing at 5 feet 5, with brown skin and a long jet black hair; double D breasts and a body that most females her age or younger would kill for.

Snapping out of his train of thoughts, Dread made his way over to the hotpot. After he got the hot water for his cup of coffee, Dread walked over to where Meeshie and True Blue were working out.

"Wats crackin cuhz?" True Blue was the first to say, after getting up from doing his set of push-ups. *"Ain't shit loco, coolin, yuh kno the vibes!"* Dread shot back, giving True Blue some dap. By now, Meeshie had gotten up from doing his set.

"Oh shit, my fault cuhz, this is the cuhz Lefty, he from my clocc too loc." True Blue said, pointing to the third nigga that was working out with them. *"Wats crackin loc,"* Lefty said. *"Wats crackin cuhz, I'm Dread."* Dread responded, giving Lefty some dap.

"Ayo cuhz , watssup! Yuh gettin this money with niggas or yuh jerkin recc?" Meeshie finally said. *"Nah loco, I have some shit to handle rite quicc."* Dread shot back. Dread went on to explain to the three of them everything that had transpired between Snoop and him without leaving anything out.

"Watever yuh want to do, yuh kno I'm with it cuhz." Meeshie was the first to say. *"I'm gon go holla at Snoop now n see watssup."* Dread stated. *"On point loco I'ma go up there to his cell now,"* he added and as he walked off in the direction of Snoop's cell.

When he got to the front of Snoop's cell, Dread knocked on the cell door. *"Come in!"* he heard Snoop say. *"Ayo Snoop, watssup?"* Dread said when he got inside of

24

Snoop's cell.*" Come on Dread I'm gone have to keep tellin yuh the same shit every day? I told yuh that Jay said that we have to wait till he go down to his visit."* Snoop shot back, getting up from his bunk.

Dread was taken aback with Snoop's response. He couldn't believe that Snoop was dead lying to him in his face. *"Green! They need yuh in 13A, the other SPA called out and yuh was next on the list."* Ms. Rodriguez said, knocking on Snoop's cell door before Dread was able to reply to Snoop's last comment.

Snoop got everything he needed for his eight hour shift. *"Yo Dread, I'm gon holla at yuh when I get back at 3.00pm,"* he added walking out of his cell, leaving dread standing in the middle of the cell. Dread shook his head before walking out of the cell. His mind was already made up with what he was going to do to Snoop.

After leaving Snoop's cell, Dread went and got on the phone. Once his girl confirmed what he already had known; he told her that he would call her back later and ended the call. Pist, his girl had told him that the money had already been picked up.

Dread ain't like how Snoop was trying to play him like he was some type of "bitch nigga". For that fact, he planned on making Snoop pay for the disrespect once he had gotten back to the unit.

By now it was already 2:45pm and almost count time. The count time was at 3.00pm; during this time, the inmates would have to be placed back in their cells until the count was clear at 4.00pm.

- - -

– After The Count –

The count cleared at exactly 4.00pm on the dot. The CO-O's came around and started unlocking and letting the inmates back out of their cells. Once Dread's door was unlocked, he wasted no time in stepping out of his cell; he had business to handle.

Snoop got dressed and stepped out of his cell. In his one hand he had his phone Book and in the other he had his Sony radio. He started making his way down the fly of stairs. As soon as he cleared the stairs, he started making his way over to the phones when he heard Dread called his name.

"Damn, this nigga again," he said to himself, but didn't turn around; he just kept walking in the direction of the phones, ignoring the fact that Dread was calling him. *"Ayo my nigga yuh dont fuckin hear me callin yuh?"* Dread

said with hostility in his voice when he finally reached where Snoop stood.

"Yo, my nigga I'm about to use the phone; holla at me when I'm done." Snoop shot back, grabbing the phone receiver off the hook. Tired of his shenanigans, Dread did what he was dying to do since this morning and took a swing at Snoop; catching him right on the left side off his face.

The off guard blow caught Snoop by surprise; causing him to drop the phone receiver. Dread took another swing but this time Snoop had side stepped it and threw one of his own, missing Dread by an inch. Dread threw another jab, followed with a right hook and hitting Snoop on his ear.

Seeing that he wasn't a match for Dread, Snoop threw two more punches before taking off running around the set of phone Booths. On the other side of the phones was Smokey, one of Dread's homies using the phone; seeing Snoop trying to make an a escape, all in one motion Smokey, rolled off the top of the garbage can that he had been sitting on, picked it up and crashed it on top of Snoop's head.

'BOOM!' Snoop, fell to the floor, but wasted no time in getting back up and making his way down the tier. By this time, the CO-O on tour had pressed the panic botton and ran inside of the bubble.

27

Right before Snoop was able to make it to the front of the unit, True Blue cut him off. Snoop took a swing at True Blue in which Snoop side stepped and threw two back of his own; making contact with Snoop's chin.

The two powerful blows by True Blue made Snoop's legs give out on him, causing him to fall to his knees; when that happened, *'Shmurda She Wrote.'* Dread, Smokey, True Blue, Wax, KD and Meeshie took turn raining blows on Snoop; all making contact with some part of Snoop's body.

Snoop was no match for the four niggas that was on him. *"Watch out cuhz!"* Wax said as he rolled the food wagon over to where the beating was taking place. Everyone cleared the way and Wax tilted the food wagon over on top of Snoop's head.

"Boom!" All the metal pans and lids fell out of the food wagon on contact. Snoop lay on the floor as if he was dead with blood pouring out from everywhere. Out of nowhere Snoop hopped up off the floor and ran toward the exit.

"Suck my dick yuh fuckin hardbacks!" Snoop shouted on his way out of the door. They tried to chase him down, but to no avail; Snoop had already shut the A and B door behind him. Snoop's blood was all over the unit's floor; it looked like a crime scene out of CSI.

Not too long after the response team had finally rushed into the unit. *"Everybody get the fuck on the ground,"* the Captain shouted. All the inmates did as they was told and laid flat on their stomachs.

Soon after, the unit was under control; and the CO-O on tour made his way back out of the bubble. The captain walked over to him and within seconds, they had the whole run down of everything that had taken place.

When it was said and done, True Blue, Meeshie, KD, Smokey, Wax and Dread were escorted out of the unit in plexy cuff; all on their way to the 'SHU' with a possible new assault charge pending over their heads.

Chapter Five

As True Blue sat in his cell, he couldn't believe how fast time has actually passed by. It's been four weeks since the incident with Snoop took place. Three days after being in the 'SHU'; all six of them had seen the lieutenant for their hearing. They all received 30days across the board.

While sitting in the box, True Blue had received one of the worst news he has ever gotten while incarcerated. While on the phone with his little man, Boo, he found out that his little man, Crandon had gotten shot and killed. True Blue couldn't believe how in a matter of six months he had lost two of his main men.

Snoop was messed up pretty bad, so bad that the jail wanted to press charges on all six of them; but luckily, Snoop had decided to stick to the street code and didn't snitch. Therefore, the jail had no other option other than to drop any pending charges against them.

While in the box, True Blue's parole had finally maxed out. After going to writ Court and signing the parole papers, the parole hold was finally lifted. Now, all he had was the $10,000 bail; and once he got out of the box, he planned on getting the ball rolling.

The last week of them being in the box, Lefty and a few others of his homies were escorted into the 'SHU' by the response team for assaulting an officer. The day they had all been waiting for has finally arrived; today would be the day that they would all be released back into population.

"Ayo True Blue!" Meeshie was heard yelling out of the side of his door. *"Ayo C, wats craccin loco?"* True Blue shot back. *"Ayo! Dread, Smokey and Wax got sent outta the buildin this mornin loco!"* Meeshie responded.

"Oh, word? Damn, that's crazy cuhz; so wat they doin with us then loco?" True Blue asked; disappointed at the fact that they had sent his men out of the building. *"They said that me, yuh n KD goin bacc to 9A"* Meeshie responded.

"Damn! Aight! Copy cuhz, I'm about to Start paccin my shit left now loco. I'ma holla at yuh once we get bacc to the crib" True Blue said before getting off of the door to go pack all his belongings.

Within the next two hours, Meeshie, KD and True Blue were packed out and sent back to their old unit; the same unit wherein they had assaulted Snoop. Being that Lefty had one of his hoes come up with $250, all that True Blue needed now was another $1,250.

The first thing True Blue did when he had gotten back in the unit was jump straight on the phone to call his Lil man, Boo. *"Ayo cuhz west crackin loco!"* True Blue said into the receiver, as soon as Boo had answered the phone.

31

"Us never them loco! Yuh kno the fuckin vibes!" Boo shot back, happy to hear that his big bro was out of the box. *"Ayo, that nigga Lil Rico home loco,"* he then added, referring to True Blue's younger brother.

"Oh word! Where the fuck that nigga at loco?" True Blue shot back, excited to hear that his little brother was home. *"That nigga had to go checc in into his parole today, but he said that he was comin bacc once he was done over there"* Boo informed True Blue.

"Copy! When he gets bacc, make sure that he know wats my bail and that I said to make sure he gets on top of that for me loco. I already got $250; all I need now is $1,250." True Blue said. *"Copy loc, say no more! I'm gone put another $250, to make that $500. And once he comes bacc I'll tell him wat yuh said cuhz."* Boo stated.

By now, the phone had beeped indicating that the call was coming to an end. *"Copy loco, say no more! C safe out there. I'll call yuh again tomorrow or something; make sure yuh take care of that for me Harlem!"* True Blue replied before the phone call was disconnected.

Chapter Six

Lil Rico has been back home for four days now; and the fact that he was still wearing the same clothes that he had on when he first came home was weighing heavy on his mind. On top of that, his brother True Blue needed him to come up with the remaining part of his bail money.

Lil Rico knew that something had to be done; he just didn't know what he would do just yet to come up with the $1,250 for True Blue's bail. There was no doubt in his mind, he wanted to do the right thing; but from the looks of it, that wasn't going to be an easy task.

Nothing has been going the way Lil Rico had expected them to go since he came home. The only good thing that happened to him since his been home was going on a date with the Dominican beauty that works in the sneaker store on east Tremont Avenue. Other than that, things were already starting to look shaky.

Not having a place to come home to was another problem, because by default he had to go parole into his mother's house in the East New York section of Brooklyn; and to add salt to the injury, he had to take the two hour train ride back and forth every day from the Bronx to Brooklyn.

Lil Rico couldn't stop thinking of ways to come up with his brother's bail money. The one thing he did know for sure, was that he was going to make sure he did everything in his power to come up with it; even if that took doing the unthinkable.

It was 10.00pm and like every other night, Lil Rico had to take the train from the Bronx back to Brooklyn. After stopping at the Ock's store to buy a pack of Newport, he then made his way to the West Farm's train station. *"Somethin have to give, bcos I dont plan on doin this shit every fuckin night,"* Lil Rico thought to himself as he walked down East Tremont on his way to the train station.

When he got to the train station, he put out his cigarette and stepped into the platform. When the train finally arrived, Lil Rico stepped inside and found the seat that he would be occupying for the next two hours.

- - -

Lil Rico reached his stop in Brooklyn at 11.00pm. When he got off the train at New Lotts Avenue, he started making his way out of the train station. When he got out of the station, he fished in his pockets for another cigarette, lit it and took a few pulls from it.

Lil Rico's mother's building was only three blocks away from the train station, giving him enough time to finish smoking his cigarette. As he passed the Bank of America on the corner of New Lotts Avenue, he couldn't believe what he had just seen. On the other side of the glass was a Spanish looking man counting what appears to be his check, in nothing but $50 bills and $20 bills.

Seeing this, a light bulb went on inside of Lil Rico's head. As his mind was already made up to the crime that he was about to commit. *"Fucc! It is either now or never,"* he thought to himself as he posted up across the street from the Bank of America.

A few minutes later, the Spanish looking man finally exited the bank and Started moving in the direction where Lil Rico was standing. When the Spanish looking man passed him, he wasted no time in going behind him and putting him in a choke hold, while pointing his finger made gun to his lower back.

Being that the block was ghost, due to the time of the night made the robbery that much easier. *"All I want is the money papi, but if yuh make me have to fight for it, then I'm gon leave yuh fightin for ya life!"* Lil Rico whispered into the man's ear.

The Spanish looking man couldn't believe why this was happening to him. His legs started shaking and his heart beat increased inside of his chest. *"Okay! Okay!! Please no hurt me!"* The Spanish looking man pleaded in a thick Spanish accent.

Reaching in his pockets, he took out the same stack of money that he had been counting and handed it to Lil Rico. Once the money was secured in his pockets, Lil Rico shoved the Spanish looking man and said *"run and yuh better not look bacc papi!"*

Without a second thought, the Spanish looking man took off running down the empty New Lotts streets. When the coast was clear, Lil Rico made his escape and disappeared like a theif in the night.

Chapter Seven

Lil Rico woke up the next morning at around 9:30am. He knew that he had moves that needed to be made and lying in bed wasn't going to cut it. Rolling out of the bed; he made his way into the small bathroom that was located right outside of his mom's room.

Being that his mom had an early appointment, he was left in the house alone. When he finished showering and taking care of all his hygiene, he made his back into his mom's room to get ready for the long day that he had ahead.

Walking over to the dresser, he picked his phone up off the charger. He had two missed calls and five unread messages; two of the messages were from OT, one from Boo and the last two from Frahelis – the same Dominican beauty that he was slowly fallen in love with.

"Oh shit!" Lil Rico said out loud after reading OT's message. With everything that took place the night before, he had forgotten all about OT coming to pick him up. Not too long after he had placed the phone back on its charger, the phone started going off again.

"Yo! Top of the morning, old head!" Lil Rico said into the receiver, already knowing who it was on the other end. *"Nigga, ya ass better be ready bcos I'm on my way*

already, I should be there in 15mins!" OT shot back disregarding, everything that Lil Rico had just said.

"Nigga, I been ready; I'm here waitin on ya old ass to get here." Lil Rico retorted, slipping on his pair of white Nike Air Force 1s. *"Aight nigga."* OT said, ending the call. Lil Rico went to place the phone back on the charger, but it started going off again; he answered on the second ring.

"Damn! Ya old ass here already nigga?" Lil Rico asked. *"Who the fucc yuh callin old nigga? The last time I checked, yuh was the only nigga on this phone!"* Boo shot back.

"Oh shit! My fault loc, I thought yuh was OT callin nigga again." Lil Rico stated when he realized that the voice on the other end was Boo's.

"Watssup tho loc, I seen ya message tellin me to call yuh." Boo said, getting straight to the point. *"Yeah loco, I was tryin to let yuh kno that I got most of the bail money for True Blue, when that nigga call give him my number n tell him to call me."* Lil Rico replied, remembering that he did in fact text Boo.   *"Copy loc, say no more. I'm gon put another to $250 on top of wat yuh n Lefty already got,"* Boo said. *"Say no more then loco; but let me get off this phone, this nigga OT callin me again he must be out front. See yuh in a few loco, thums!"* Lil Rico said before ending the call.

After grabbing everything he needed, Lil Rico left out of his mom's house; locking the door behind him, he started making his way down the stairs. When he got to the front of the building, he spotted OT's Lincoln Navigator sitting idle by the fire hydrant.

"Damn OT, this muther fuccer here nice!" Lil Rico said stepping into the truck; his body sunk into the leather seats immediately. Lil Rico had met OT a few years back; OT was one of his best customers at the time. During the time that OT had spent copping off of Lil Rico, they had built a good father and son relationship.

Although OT was what most would call a feen, he was far from the average feen. OT always stayed in the latest designers, nice cars, money in his pockets, and was fucking some of the 'baddest' bitches around. He did the drugs and did not allow the drugs to do him.

"Shit, if yuh think this bitch bad now, wait till I finish gettin this muther fuccer all the way tuned up!" OT shot back, putting the truck in gear and pulling off of the curve. *"Shit, this shit looks good as it is to me!"* Lil Rico responded.

The inside of the truck looked like a spaceship. The smell of new leather was evident in the truck. The small 13 inch screen TV on the dash board played the latest rap videos. While the lyrics came thumping out of the truck surround system.

"Wats the plans for today OT?" Lil Rico queried. *"I need to make a few moves, but first, I need to stop at the bank. Then I'm gone take yuh where yuh need to go so that I can bust my moves,"* OT responded, navigating the truck into the Jacky Robinson Park way.

"Nigga! We just passed a bank by my mom's blocc." Lil Rico said, confused. He was referring to the same Bank of America where he had caught the Spanish man for his check the night before. *"Yeah, I kno, but I rather wait till we get to the BX, so I can hit the bank on East Tremont."* OT calmly said. Lil Rico just shook his head, and got comfortable in his seat.

"So wats ya plans now that yuh home nigga?" OT asked, putting the volume down. *"Shit, before I do anything, I need to get my brother out of jail. Once that's done, then I'll focus on wat I'm goin to be doin in the long run."* Lil Rico answered, meaning every word spoken. OT glanced over at him for a few seconds before putting his focus back on the road.

OT and Lil Rico arrived in the Bronx at exactly 12:45pm. When they got to East Tremont, OT navigated the truck to the Chase Bank that was located in the corner of Author Avenue and East Tremont.

"Yo, watch my shit, if the Police comes, just move my shit. Don't let my shit get a ticket nigga." OT said before jumping out of the truck and walking into the Chase Bank. Lil Rico took this time to hit his shorty up and let her know that he was on his way to her store, to cop a new pair of sneaker. Thereafter, he called Boo and told him to meet him in the sneaker store called 'Sneaker Freaker'.

Ten minutes later, OT walked out of the bank and jumped into the driver seat. Putting the truck in gear, he made the illegal U-turn and made his way back up East Tremont. Two minutes later, OT was parking in front of the 'Sneaker Freaker' store.

"Nigga, I have to bust this move, but I'll be back later to take yuh back to BK. Make sure yuh ready when I come or ya ass gone be takin that long ass train ride." OT said, double parkin in front of 'Sneaker Freaker'. *"Copy loco, I'll be ready when yuh spin bacc around for me."* Lil Rico said as he released his seatbelt. Before he was able to step out of the truck, OT stopped him in his tracks.

"Look nigga, I see that ya mind is on gettin ya brother out. I don't want yuh to do no dumb shit for the bread. Yuh said that his bail was $1,500 n that yuh already

41

got a band. So look, this wat I'm gon do for yuh. I'm gon give yuh this $500, just make sure yuh give that shit back once y'all get on ya feet." OT said catching Lil Rico by surprise.

OT loved Lil Rico as if he was his own and he would hate to see him go back to jail knowing that he could have helped him. Reaching in his pockets, he pulled off five $100 bills and then handed it to Lil Rico.

"Thank yuh OT, yuh kno we gon make sure yuh get ya money back." Lil Rico said, givin OT some dap before jumping out of the truck. When he got out of the truck, Lil Rico walked into the 'Sneaker Freaker'.

Chapter Eight

True Blue woke up the next morning feeling good about the day he had ahead. After speaking to his brother Lil Rico the night before, all his worries was no longer an issue. The bail money too was no longer the issue, now it was just all a waiting game; a game True Blue didn't have the patience to play.

Rolling out of his bunk, True Blue walked over to the toilet and emptied his bladder. Afterwards, he washed his hands and began to brush his teeth after he had washed his face. Looking out of his cell door window, he noticed that it was 8:35am on the clock that hung off the dayroom wall.

"Damn, I need to hurry up," True Blue said to himself when he remembered that he and Meeshie had planned on going to the yard to get a few sets of pull ups. When he was done taking care of his cell and his hygiene, True Blue gave his cell door the special knock so that the CO-O on duty can come and let him out.

A few minutes passed before the CO-O finally came to let him out of his cell. *" On the yard! On the yard!"* The yard CO-O came through the doors yelling; everyone that was going to the yard Started exiting the unit and those that weren't stood in the dayroom politicking.

43

All True Blue wanted to do was go to the yard to kill some time. When he returns from the yard, he had plans to call Lil Rico back to see if he was up and ready. Shortly after True Blue and Meeshie finished doing their sets, the CO-O came into the yard to inform the inmates that their rec was over.

The time now was 10:45am. When all the inmates had exited the yard, they were escorted back to their housing unit. True Blue wasted no time on going to get on the phone. He picked up the phone receiver and placed a call to his brother, Lil Rico.

The phone rang twice on the other end before Lil Rico finally answered. *"This call is being recorded and monitored ...,"* the operator said before allowing the call to finally go through. *"Ayo C! Wats up cuhz, talk to me nice, wat its lookin like."* True Blue shot anxiously into the receiver once the call was put through.

"West craccin loco, top of the morning; n ain't shit loco, we gat the bailsbond shit left now, takin care of the paper work. Once that's taken care of, yuh good to go!" Lil Rico responded. Smile spread across True Blue's face as the words left Lil Rico's mouth.

"Oh Okay! Copy that! I'm gon let yuh go then loco n let yuh get bacc to wat yuh was doin. I'll call yuh bacc later

44

to see watssup." True Blue said. . Lil Rico said. *"Thank yuh loco! Real nigga shit!"* True Blue retorted.

"Nigga stop ya shit, yuh dont have to thank me for doin wat I'm supposed to be doin!" Lil Rico shot back, slightly offended by True Blue's last comment. *"Yeah, yuh right loc, love yuh cuhz. I'll call yuh bacc later."* After the call ended, True Blue made his way over to where Meeshie was sitting at.

"Wats the word loco, wats Lil Rico talkin about?" Meeshie asked True Blue once he was close enough. *"Shit that nigga said he was at the bailsbond man's; and now takin care of all the paper work!"* True Blue answered excitedly. By now, he could taste his freedom at the tip of his tongue.

"Littisha! That's watssup loc. But on a more serious note loc, I need yuh to go home n do the left thin. Shit, the gang already in here, we need yuh out there loco, please go out there n do the left thin." Meeshie said, with a look of seriousness.

"Yeah. I kno loco, I'm off parole so that shit aint gon be hard to do now. Yuh kno yuh n the crodies can always call me for anything. If i got it, y'all got it!" True Blue said, looking at Meeshie directly in his eyes meaning every word spoken.

After Meeshie and True Blue had finished their heart to heart conversation, True Blue went into his cell to get ready to jump in the shower. After he had showered, True Blue threw on a pair of all blue basketball shorts and his matching all black GV Special Puma sneakers.

Making his way out of his cell, True Blue walked over to the hot pot to get some hot water for his cup of coffee. Spotting Meeshie and KD playing a game of casino a few tables away, he made his way towards them.

"Nigga, wat yuh doin over here! Yuh dont want none of this shit here!" KD said as True Blue took a seat on the table. *"Shit, nigga yuh can't even handle Meeshie. Wat makes yuh think yuh can handle me nigga?"* True Blue shot back defensively.

"Fucc out of here! This nigga bout to get glove!" KD retorted. *"Nah, I dont believe that shit."* True Blue said. *"Nah, he aint lyin loco,"* Meeshie finally said, *"today not my day loc, thats all,"* he then added. A few minutes passed and just like KD had said, Meeshie had gotten gloved.

It wasn't over yet for KD though; he went on to talk shit until him and True Blue Started another game of casino. *"Nigga, dont think yuh gone glove me, that's not happenin!"* True Blue said, throwing the queen of spades onto the table.

"*Nigga, I'm gon do yuh just like I just did Meeshie, y'all both gone have matchin gloves walkin around here lookin like Micheal Jaccin*" KD bragged; and they both burst into laughter. They went on to play three more games of casino: two – one was the score; True Blue's way.

"*Yuh luccy I dont feel like doin yuh like that today.*" True Blue said getting up from the table they were sitting at. Within minutes, all three of them made their way up to the upper tier to get their smoke on. Before they knew it, it was lock-in time and all the inmates were placed back into their cell's until the count was clear.

- - -

– After The Count –

It was 4.00pm and the count had finally cleared. For some reasons, out of all days, today, the count time felt like it took longer than it normally did to clear. For True Blue, stepping out of his cell, he made his way back toward the phones.

Picking up the phone receiver, True Blue dial Lil Rico's number and impatiently waited for him to answer. "*This call is being recorded and monitored,*" the operator said before allowing the call to go through.

"*Wats craccin cuhz,*" Lil Rico said. "*Ain't shit here, just locced bacc out now; Wat happen earlier? How's*

47

everythin goin?" True Blue asked getting straight to the point. *"Yeah, everythin gucci loco, yuh should be out of there today, before the day is over cuhz ."* Lil Rico replied.

"Oh, okay copy! Loco I cant wait to get outta this bitch! Oh, n Meeshie sent his blue passion too." True Blue said. *"Oh word! Tell that nigga that I sent mine round trip cuhz; make sure yuh give that nigga my info beforr yuh leave too."* Lil Rico responded. *"I got yuh cuhz."*

By now, the phone had beeped indicating that the call was coming to an end. The brothers said their goodbyes and promised to link back up once True Blue was a free man again.

- - -

– Home Sweet Home–

True Blue woke up the next day in his mother's house. Although he was only gone for three months, he felt like he hadn't slept in a real mattress in years. By the time True Blue had finished showering and getting dressed it was 9:30am.

When he made it out of the door of his mom's apartment, he placed a call to Lil Rico before leaving; they both agreed to meet up on 149st. and Grand Concourse in the Bronx on the two and the five train.

Since the train was going express, it only took him one hour to get to 149st. and Grand Concourse from Lefrak City in Queens NY. A few trains passed and Lil Rico was still nowhere in sight. When the next train had finally arrived and came to a stop on 149st, True Blue scanned the train for his brother. Luckily, Lil Rico was in fact on this train.

Walking over to his brother, True Blue embraced him into a manly hug. *"Damn crodie, I see that shocc shit got yuh out here lookin like Bruce Lee."* True Blue said. *"Shit, them nigga be havin nigga workin out at 5.00am every morning loco. I better be lookin like something."* Lil Rico shot back.

The train ride from 149st and Grand Concourse to East Tremont and West Farm Square was a 25 minute train ride. When the train had finally came to a stop at West Farm Square, True Blue and Lil Rico exited the train into the nice summer weather.

It was a 10 minute walk from West Farm Square to East Tremont and Hughes Avenue. Once they reached the corner of East Tremont and Hughes Avenue, Lil Rico was the first to spot Boo, Reddot and the nigga he met the day he came home named Legend all standing in front of big homie Deli's grocery store.

49

"*Gllllllllltttttttttttt!!!*" True Blue shouted once he had spotted Boo and Reddot as well. "*Pow! Pow!*" Boo shot back in return, turning around to face them. "*Wats craccin cuhz! Welcome home nigga!*" Reddot said as True Blue and Lil Rico had reached the corner.

"*Good lookin cuhz! Wat y'all niggas fuccin wit?*" True Blue shot back, after giving Reddot and Boo some dap. "*Yo cuhz, this right here is my man Legend that I was tellin yuh about,*" Boo said, pointing in Legend's direction.

"*Oh, okay! Copy that loco, wats craccin cuhz!*" True Blue greeted Legend. "*Ain't shit loco, coolin, I heard a lot of good thing about y'all. I'm happy that y'all finally home.*" Legend responded; happy to finally meet the famous brothers. "*Yeah, tell me about it; a nigga was tired of sittin in that shit fr fr.*" True Blue said.

Boo was the youngest of them all; at 18 years young, he stood at 5 feet 7, 145lbs, mid-light skin complexion, low ceaser haircut, with tattoos covering both of his arms and some of his upper body. Boo was a money getter that only liked to use violent when it's needed.

Reddot on the other hand was 26 years young, he stood 5 feet 5, 180lbs, brown skin, with a few tattoos spread throughout his body including his facial area and cornrows to the back of his neck. Reddot was the true definition of a true savage. Reddot lived for the drama and never thought twice about busting a cop on a nigga.

Legend was 23 years old, the same age as True Blue and Lil Rico, but unlike them, he stood 5 feet 9, 165lbs, his skin color was like the color of a brown paper bag; and he had thick waves in his ceaser cut. Legend was the weed plug on Hughes Avenue; anything you wanted from quarter to ounces or pounds, he had it.

Shortly after True Blue and Lil Rico pulled up to the block, the five of them went into Legend's apartment which was located right on 178th and Hughes Avenue. The mother land of the 'Rollin 30s' neighborhood Crip set in the Bronx.

As soon as they were in the apartment, blunts of weed Started going in the air nonstop. Legend had half of gallon of Hennessey left from the night before; and that too was now in rotation. True Blue had smoke so many blunts that night that he ended up passing out on the couch that rested in the corner of Legend's room before midnight.

- - -

– The Next Day –

The next day, True Blue woke with a hang over, but that didn't stop him from getting the ball rolling. Now that he was home, the only thing he had in mind was to get to the top by any means necessary.

Chapter Nine

True Blue and Lil Rico had been home for almost a month and they were already playing the block heavy. After getting the call from his man 'E', True Blue went to go meet up with him and came back with 100 bundles of some raw dope.

The fiends couldn't seem to be getting enough of it, as the traffic in Hughes was like no other. E had told True Blue that he ain't want nothing back for it; but the two had agreed to take the money they made back to 'E' and re-up with.

On this particular morning, the sun was out and there was very little to no breeze; to make it worst there wasn't no shade also. Lil Rico had a pair of white v-neck t-shirt, all blue Nike sweat shorts with his fresh out the box white up towns.

Lil Rico, True Blue and Boo were posted on the corner of big homies Deli on trap Star mode. The fiends were coming from every angle. The work was so good that they were even traveling over from other blocks trying to get their hands on the new checker's.

Due to the glassine having the checker board patterns, the fiend named it 'Checkers.' To avoid going back and forth to Brooklyn; Lil Rico and True Blue decided to crash in Legend's apartment for the time being; of which Legend didn't mind, not one bit. In fact, he liked having the brothers around.

"Ayo loco, how much work yuh got left?" True Blue asked Lil Rico when he got back from serving a fiend. *"I'm almost out loc, I'm down to my last three bundles."* Lil Rico responded as he stuffed the money he had gotten from his sale into his pockets. *"Niggas need some more of this shit ASAP cuhz!"* he said further.

"Yuh ain't never lie loco, that's wat I'm tryin to do right now fr fr." True Blue shot back; already thinking the same thing Lil Rico was thinking. *"The last time I seen the blocc this litt was when niggas was out here wit that flow,"* he added.

'Flow' was the name of the previous stamp that they had on the block. Flow at the time was one of the best dope around. *"Ayo Boo! C6 comin up the blocc loco!"* Lil Rico called out to Boo letting him know that a squat car was making its way up the block.

Boo made the sale before the cruiser made it to the corner. When the cruiser had finally reached the corner, True Blue, Boo and Lil Rico were already inside of Legend's apartment. They had been posted on the corner since 6.00am and felt like it was time to take a break and disappear from the scene for a little while.

"Yo cuhz, let me get that bread, I'm tryin to go see E right now," True Blue said reaching in his pockets and taking out all the money that he made in the few hours that he had spent at the corner; just as he finished counting the money, Lil Rico also reached in his pockets and handed True Blue the stack of money that he had in his own pockets.

True Blue and Boo rolled up and began to have their little smoke section. Legend's room smelled like loud in no time. Being that Lil Rico had already started his parole, he wasn't smoking. In between blunts, True Blue placed a call to E; after telling E that he was on his way over, he ended the call.

- - -

– Harlem New York –

"Ayo Royd, this nigga True Blue on his way over here, he said that they were done with those 100 things already." E said still not being able to believe that True Blue was already done with the 100 bundles he had given him just four days ago.

"Damn! Didn't yuh just give him that shit four days ago?" Royd asked, stepping into the living room with a surprise look on his face as well. *"Yeah bro, but I ain't gone sit here and act like he ain't say that the shit would be gone*

in no time. He did say that his block was a gold mine." E said, lighting the freshly rolled blunt.

E and Royd sat across from each other on the living room table. The two began to get True Blue's order ready for when he arrives while they smoke on some of the best weed around.

- - -

– H-Blocc –

True Blue made it back to the Bronx safe and sound in an hour. After paying the cab drive, True Blue stepped out of the cab with a small Book bag in hand. Stepping into Legend's building '620', he made his way over to Legend's apartment's door; when he entered into Legend's room, he found Boo, Legend and Lil Rico playing a game of call of duty on the big flat screen TV.

"Damn, that was fast cuhz!" Lil Rico was the first to say, without taking his eyes of the TV. *"Shit, Harlem is right across the bridge nigga."* True Blue shot back dumping everything that the Book bag held inside onto Legend's bed. By now, the three had focused their attention toward the bed.

What came out of the Book bag was a bulletproof vest, two 9mm hand guns and 200 bundles of dope. *"Damn, where the fucc yuh get all this shit from cuhz!"* Lil Rico said excitedly as he picked up the all black 9mm Baretta.

"Shit, E said that now that we about to Start getting his money, that we better off stayin safe than sorry." True Blue shot back nonchalantly. Legend got up from where he was seated and made his way over towards the bed; picking up the 9mm Rugar he Stared at it for a while before a smile spread across his face.

Boo on the other hand threw the bullet proof vest over his head and Started posing in front of Legend's mirror. All True Blue could do was smile at how his men were acting with their new toys.

"Look, I have to go meet my lil bitch Christal tonight, so I'm about to go see Flaco so he can hook me up with a fresh cut." True Blue finally said after he had split the 200 bundles evenly with Lil Rico.

True Blue was so focused on getting the ball rolling on his plans that the last thing on his mind was getting some pussy; but now that the ball was finally in motion, he decided to finally get his dick out the mud.

- - -

– Uptown, the Bronx –

True Blue made it to the uptown section of the Bronx where Christal lives at around 9:30pm. After getting out of the cab, True Blue took his phone out and gave Christal a call. She answered on the second ring.

"Hey sexy, I'm out front," True Blue said into the receiver. *"Okay love, I'll be right out."* Christal responded before ending the call. In a few minutes, she was at the front door with nothing on but a pair of boy's shorts that had her camel toe on full display.

Christal's upper body was covered also only with the tank top she was wearing with no bra on; her nipples poking out of the fabric. True Blue's dick slowly stated growing in his pants.

"Damn ma, yuh lookin good enough to eat in them shorts; wat yuh tryin to do to a nigga?" True Blue said embracing her into a tight hug while his hands palmed her soft big juicy round ass.

"Mmm," Christal let out a soft moan, loving the way True Blue's hands felt on her body. *"I'm tryin to do nothing to yuh hunny, at least not just yet!"* Christal said; stepping to the side so that True Blue can come inside her apartment.

As soon as they entered inside of the apartment, the horny lovebirds wasted no time as they started to tear each other's clothes off; in a flash, the two of them were as naked as they were the day they were born.

True Blue slowly placed Christal on the couch lifted her legs up and made his way down south until he was face to face with Christal's love box. He hadn't touched her yet, but she was already dripping wet just at the thought of what True Blue was about to do her.

"Damn daddyy!!!" she let out a moan as True Blue's lips made contact with her second pair of lips. He sucked, licked, and kissed on her pussy, loving the way the pussy tasted in his mouth. True Blue was eating her pussy like if it was the last meal on planet earth.

True Blue held Christal's legs into her chest as he went to work on her pussy. *"I'm-I'mmmm cu-cuuu-cuummmiinnn!"* Christal moaned decorating True Blue's face with her thick white cum. True Blue wasn't done with her yet as he turned her around on all four; he place one of the couch pillows under her stomach and told her to arch her back.

True Blue stroked his dick, pre-cum oozing out of the mushroom shaped head as he looked at how wet Christal's pussy was; not being able to take it anymore, True Blue stuck his dick into Christal's pussy inch by inch until all seven and a half inches were deep inside of her pussy.

"ohhhhhhhh!!!!!! daddddyyy! Ya dick feeeelss so-s-so-so goooddd!" she moaned. True Blue and Christal ended up fucking in every position on her living room couch until they both had repeated back to back orgasms.

Chapter Ten

In the shorts two months that Legend had known True Blue and Lil Rico, he had grown a lot of respect and love for them. He liked the way they moved; they were loyal to core and about that life in every aspect.

Ever since they came home, Legend witnessed the block make a change for the better. Before their return, the money was coming but not as much as it was now that True Blue and Lil Rico was home. The block was jumping and that only meant one thing; money was coming in hand over fist.

"Ayo Boo, not for nothing but I really fucc's with True Blue n Lil Rico. I'm thinkin about lettin them rent out the bacc room, so that they can be here on the blocc with us instead of havin to go bacc n forth to Brooklyn n shit," Legend said, taking a few puffs out of the blunt he and Boo had been smoking on.

"Yeah loco, I told yuh that once they got home, shit was gon be a lot different, them my big bros loco n they really carry H-Blocc on their bacc alone with this Crip shit." Boo said as he took the blunt that Legend was passing to him.

"Yeah, I fuccs with them the long way," Legend declared just before his phone rang which he answered on

the second ring. *"Yo, watssup playa?"* he said. *"Yo Legend, yuh around?"* the voice on the other end asked.

"Yuh kno I am, why would I not be, if this is where the money is at?" Legend shot back licking the freshly rolled blunt close and then lighting it. *"I need to come see yuh, I want the usual."* the voice said.

"I'm here; pull up, yuh kno where to find me." Legend responded taking a few more puffs of the blunt before passing it to Boo. *"Aight bet."* Legend ended the call and threw his phone back on the bed.

"Ayo Boo, I'll be right back. I'm about to go bust this chop. Set the game up bcos I'm comin bacc inside to smoke yuh in some fight night nigga!" Legend said, grabbing the two eights for his customer. *"Nigga, yuh aint sayin nothin! Dont threaten me with a good time nigga!"* Boo retorted, turning the PS4 on.

Legend stepped out of the room and walked out of the apartment. After he had served his customer he made his way back into the apartment and into the room within a short time. *"Nigga $50 a match!"* Legend said, taking a seat next to Boo. *"Nigga shoot $100! Yuh gettin money aint yuh?"* Boo shot back sarcastically. *"Yuh aint sayin nothin nigga! Thats a bet!"*

Chapter Eleven

The weather was nice out. The sun wasn't too hot, there was enough shade and breeze making the summer day feel nice and cool. Lil Rico, True Blue, Legend and Boo sat in front of the building 620 enjoying the nice summer day; smoking, drinking and serving every fiend that came to cop their fix.

"Ayo watssup with them Belmont niggas?" Lil Rico asked taking a sip out of his fifth of Hennessey. Being that he was on parole, he decided to fall back on the weed and choose to sip on some dark liquor on this particular day.

"I don't kno, them nigga be up there gettin money, they fake got a lil flow with the cracc, dope and coke." Boo said taking the blunt Legend was passing him. *"Oh word!"* True Blue finally said.

"Shit, them niggas gon have to Start coppin from us, because I'm not heat wavin them niggas bein right up the blocc, sellin shit cuttin niggas throat." Lil Rico said, feeling the effects of the Hennessey kicking in. Although he was feeling nice, he meant every word he had just spoken.

"I'm sayin I'm with whatever ya'll tryin to do crody!" Legend said, rubbing his hands together. *"Shit! Fucc sittin here talkin about it, let's go let it be fuccin known!"* True Blue shot back, getting up from the spot in where he

was just sitting at. He wasn't with all the talking; for him, it's either they were going to do it or stop talking about it.

- - -

– Up the Block, Belmont Ave –

Cavs, C-Lite and Montana sat in front of C-Lite's building smoking while taking care of all the incoming traffic. *"Damn, the block litty today tribu,"* said stuffing the $50 he had just gotten from a fiend in his pockets. *"Yeah, shit deff clickin today. I aint even gon front; Niggas gone be done before 5.00pm hits."* Cavs shot back agreeing with C-Lite.

"Who them niggas comin up the block?" Montana asked seeing the four niggas making their way up the block in their direction. Cavs and C-Lite directed their attention to where Montana was looking.

"Oh, thats them H-Blocc niggas; the one in the middle is True Blue and the one in the left with the blue is Lil Rico. They brothers and they just came home I heard," C-Lite said. *"Fuck them niggas comin over for?"* Cavs queried; his gut feeling already telling him that something was off.

"I don't kno tribu, but we about to find out." C-Lite shot back. At this time, the H-Blocc niggas were only inches away. *"Wats the word C-Lite!"* Lil Rico said once he was close enough to the three.

64

"Ain't shit bro, cool n tryin to get this money. Welcome home by the way," C-Lite shot back not trying to make any eye contact with Lil Rico. *"Good lookin! Good lookin! But, about that money shit; that's wat we here for now,"* Lil Rico retorted, getting straight to the point.

"Wat about that money shit?" Cavs finally said, not liking the way Lil Rico was talking. *"Oh! It's simple,"* True Blue Started to say, *"I'm gon put it to y'all like this; I kno y'all over here getting a lot of money and bein that we right down the blocc, shit been comin up short in our end. So, we came up with the idea that y'all should Start getting ya work from us."* True Blue added.

"Why the fuck would we do that? We good the way we are now; we dont work for nobody!" Cavs, the fat one out the three retorted defensively. *"Well, too bad we aint tryin to hear that loco; we came over here with our mind made up, so it's either that or we gon make it very uncomfortable for y'all to be out here eatin,"* Lil Rico interrupted.

The whole time, neither C-Lite nor Montana said a word. They already knew firsthand how True Blue and Lil Rico got down. They wanted no part of it; if it was up to them they would have had already taken their offer and go on with their day. But Cavs on the other hand wasn't trying to go for all that; he was a man and he stood on his own feet.

"Niggas gon give y'all till friday to think about this When we come bacc, I hope y'all made up y'all mind because if not, shit might get ugly fr fr." Legend finally said pointing his trigger finger in his chin for some action.

Boo just stood off to the side with hand in his Nike sweat shorts wrapped around the butt of the 9mm Rugar. *"Well, y'all might as well dont even come back because the answer gon stay the same; Friday, next Friday and the Friday after next!"* Cavs shot back. *"We aint goin for none of that!"* he then added, holding his ground.

"Copy! Say no more tuff guy; we would see wat happens when we spin bacc around then. I hope yuh keep that same energy." True Blue said stepping into Cavs space. With that being said, they turned around and started making their way off the block.

"Yuh think them niggas gone fall in line?" Boo asked once they had reached the corner of Hughes and East Tremont. *"I don't kno loco, but if they knew wat was best for them; they would."* True Blue responded.

- - -

– Friday, 8.00PM –

"Ayo cuhz, I aint even gone lie; if them niggas aint tryin to fall in line, I'm gon set an example." Reddot said as he

loaded his 9mm up with hollow tips, meaning every word. *"Nah, them nigga kno better, they gone fall right in line. If not, then do wat yuh do best loco."* True Blue was the first to say.

As soon as the sun had completely set, True Blue, Lil Rico, Reddot, Legend and Boo departed Legend's apartment on their way to Belmont Avenue, the next block over. Cavs, C-Lite and Montana were in their usual spot in front of their building on trap Star mode.

Montana was the first one to spot the five figures making their way up the block in their direction. *"Ah man, there them niggas come,"* Montana said as his heartbeat started increasing inside of his chest. Both C-Lite and Cavs turned to look in the same direction that Montana was looking in.

"Man, them niggas better not be comin over here on no dumb shit because I ain't goin for none of that!" Cavs declared, ready for whatever or at least he thought he was. *"Wats craccin, talk to me nice? Y'all niggas decided wat y'all gon do yet?"* Lil Rico said with sarcasm in his voice as he looked at the three friends head to toe.

"Nah, we haven't, Lil Rico," C-Lite responded avoiding eye contact with Lil Rico. *"Oh, so y'all niggas thought we was playin, I see!"* True Blue added. *"Man, fuck!*

..." Cavs was trying to say, but the slug that came out of Reddot's 9mm pierced through his knee cap stopping him mid-sentence.

Cavs fell to the floor holding his knee as the blood sipped through his fingers. C-Lite and Montana looked like they were ready to run off and leave their man behind. *"Try it, and see how far y'all make it."* Legend said with a smile on his face, as he pointed the 9mm Rugar in their direction; none of them moved though.

"Both of y'all niggas strip the fucc down, take everythin out y'all poccets, if I find anything in y'all pockets, it's gone be a fuccin problem! All y'all niggas had to do was fall in line, but nah, y'all wanted to be tuff guys. Now look at yuh!" True Blue stated, looking in Cavs' direction that was now on the floor bleeding and in pain.

Not wanting to get shot, Montana and C-Lite did as they were told. When they had handed Boo everything out of their pockets, Legend made his way over to where Cavs was laying on the floor, stepping over him, he started going in his pockets.

"Talk all that tuff shit now fat boii! Ya bitch ass! Give me all this shit nigga!" Legend was saying as he emptied Cavs' money and drugs from his pockets. When he was

satisfied he stood up and kicked Cavs right on his freshly shot knee.

"Aahhhhhhhhh!!!" Cavs let out a moan. The police siren could be heard getting closer and closer. *"Shut ya bitch ass up! I don't want to see none of y'all niggas out here gettin any money if is not our work or y'all aint payin dues to nigga."* Lil Rico said; and just like that the statement was made.

The five of them made their way out of Belmont Avenue like nothing ever happened. All together they came up with $5,000 in cash and little over $4,600 in work; but they could have cared less about the money and the work, they wanted one thing and one thing only – Belmont Avenue.

Chapter Twelve

– A Few Days Later –

True Blue walked out of Flaco's barber shop on East TRemont feeling like new money. It's been a few days since the incident had taken place on Belmont Avenue and the word already had gotten out as to who was responsible for it – the 'H-Blocc Niggas'.

The news of Cavs getting shot was still the topic in the barber shop, like it had happened the day before. *"I heard wat y'all niggas did to them Belmont Niggas,"* Flaco had said, as he was cutting True Blue's hair. Flaco had been True Blue's barber for as long as he could remember. Before Flaco, it was JC.

Even though Flaco was trustworthy, True Blue still wasn't trying to discuss the other day's events with him. So he decided to not say anything in return. True Blue was shocked at how fast the word had gotten out. Due to the heat that Cavs' getting shot brought, they all had decided to lay low for a few days.

True Blue reached into his pockets for his phone and placed a call to Legend. *"Yo loco, I'm on my way down TRemont to go get me a new trap phone loco,"* True Blue said into the receiver when Legend answered.

70

"Aight loco, copy! But just wait for us we rollin wit yuh; yuh kno we need to all travel together. Better safe than sorry," Legend shot back, making a point. *"Copy cuhz, I'm here in front of Flaco's right now."* True Blue stated.

Flaco's barbershop was directly across the street from Belmont Avenue, but ever since the incident had taken place, the block has been empty. A few minutes passed and Legend, Boo and Lil Rico finally pulled up.

The weather was nice. All four of them, except for True Blue, had on a pair of basketball shorts, white v-neck t-shirts with a pair of some fresh white Nike. True Blue had on his feet a pair of Jordan slippers to complete his outfit.

True Blue had his 38. Special Snub Nose tucked away in his boxer briefs and Lil Rico had his 380. in the same place. They have vowed to never leave the crib without their hammers since the incident with Cavs had taken place.

The four of them entered the Boost Mobile store on East Tremont and Clinton. The store was empty so they figured that they wouldn't be there for long. *"Hey y'all, wat yuh guys doin down here?"* The girl behind the counter asked. Her name was Jessica and she was also a Crip.

"West craccin loca! A nigga need a new trap phone," True Blue was the first to say, walking over to the counter

71

giving Jessica a kiss on the cheek. Boo, Lil Rico and Legend did the same.

"Oh, okay that aint about nothing! Yuh kno I got yuh cuhz!." Jessica responded as she made her way toward the back of the store to get True Blue the trap phone he wanted. While they waited on Jessica's return the door to the shop had open. A male wearing all blue entered the store and made his was over to where Lil Rico was standing.

"West craccin Lil Rico? Long time dont see cuhz!" The male wearing all blue said to Lil Rico. *"Oh shit, west craccin cuhz? Yuh kno how this shit goes; a nigga just came home not too long ago."* Lil Rico responded recognizing the male in blue.

The male in blue turned around and greeted Boo and Legend as well. Walking over to True Blue he said, *"West craccin cuhz!"* True Blue looked up and shook his head; he couldn't believe that the nigga in front of him actual had the balls to approach him on some Crip shit.

"Nigga fucc out my face pussy! Yuh aint no Crip of mine nigga! With ya low ridin ass!" True Blue said. The term *'low ridin'* was used only when a Crip member would only claim Crip when he's around his own, but when he's around his enemies he acts like he ain't a Crip.

The man standing in front of him was Blue Heff. True Blue and Blue Beff had done some time on Rikers Island a few years back. They were both in the same unit until the morning that Blue Heff had gotten packed up and sent out of the building to another building, C95.

Unbeknown to Blue Heff, word had gotten back to True Blue that once he was packed out of the building and was sent to the five building, that he was placed inside a blood unit and he was no longer claiming Crip.

True Blue got up from the little stool that he had been sitting on. *"Nigga! Yuh got me fucced up! I'm Crip! Who the fucc yuh think yuh are nigga? Yuh aint my CIG homie nigga!"* Blue Heff retorted.

"Oh no cuhz! Please take that outside, not in the store y'all gon get me fired!" Jessica came out of the back and interrupted. Not minding Jessica, True Blue reached inside of his basketball shorts for his 38; seeing the move, Blue Heff took flight out of the store.

"Damn that nigga fast!" Legend said looking in the direction that Blue Heff took off in. *"Yo cuhz, I'll be bacc for that phone in a few,"* True Blue said aggravated; before he was able to make his way out of the store his iPhone rung in his pockets.

"Yo, west up loca talk to me nice." True Blue said as he answered his phone; after hearing what the person on the other end of the receiver had said, he said. *"Copy loca I'm in Clinton and East Tremont. Pull up on me."* When he ended the call, he walked out of the store in the same direction Blue Heff had run on his way to Fairmont Avenue – Blue Heff's block.

When the five of them had reached the corner of Clinton and Fairmont, True Blue spotted a small crowd posted next to an all-black Nissan Altima. The windows were rolled down as 'Ooouuuu' by the female rapper – Young MA pumped out of the speakers.

Stepping in the middle of the block True Blue shouted. *"Ayo, where Blue Heff at?"* No one seemed to hear him, so he repeated himself. *"Ayo, where Blue Heff at?"* This time, he caught the attention of one of the niggas that was standing by the Nissan.

When the nigga saw who the voice had belong to, he and everyone around the car ducked off behind the Nissan. Seeing this surprised True Blue, unknown to True Blue, Blue Heff had gone back and told them that he had been jumped by the H-Blocc niggas.

From all the way down the block, True Blue had noticed that the trunk of the Nissan was popped open. *"Fucc y'all nigga poppin trunks for?"* True Blue said already knowing the answer. He reached inside of his basketball short for his gun. When he spotted a pair of hands reaching inside of the trunk, he brought out his 38. and let rip in the direction of the Nissan.

BOOM!

BOOM!

BOOM!

Without wasting any time Lil Rico followed suit; bringing his 380. to life as well.

BOC!

BOC!

BOC!

The first four shots blew the back windows of the Nissan out, as well as the passenger side windows; the hollows from the 38. and the 380. rocked the car back and forth.

TAT!

TAT!

TAT!

TAT!

Four shots from a small caliber hand gun was heard coming out from behind the Nissan. *BOOM!* True Blue let off another shot. Not wanting to get pinned up behind the Nissan, the small crowd that was behind the Nissan tried to make a run inside their building.

When the first head was exposed, True Blue let of his final shot, out of his six-shot handgun, hitting his target dead at the center of his back; making him fall face first into the pavement.

When the shooter that was behind the Nissan observed that True Blue was out of bullets, he tried to go in for the kill. He stood up exposing his body; a mistake that would cost him nothing but his life.

BOC!

BOC!

BOC!

Seeing the move, Lil Rico let his 380. spit nothing but lead out the barrel. The first bullet found a home in the chest of the shooter. The second bullet caught him on his shoulder; and last final bullet caught him dead in his face, killing him before he hit the floor.

By now, the Police siren could be heard getting closer by the minute. Not wanting to get caught on the scene, with two hot guns, True Blue, Legend, Lil Rico and Boo made their escape; but not before stopping in the mid of the block, to drop the guns off in AR's car.

AR was True Blue's lil' homie and she was the one who had called him when he was at the Boost Mobile store. She was in the army and was licensed to carry. Being that she was in the force the chances of her getting stopped and searched was one in a million; which is why True Blue had chosen to have her drive the hot guns back to H-Blocc.

They all made it back to H-Blocc without any issues and not too long after they had gotten there, AR pulled up with the two hot but empty guns in her car. Just like True Blue had expected, her car didn't even get stopped or looked at twice by the NYPD.

This was the beginning of a war that would claim the life of a lot of good niggas. One thing for sure and two things for certain; H-BLOCC had every intension of coming out on top.

Chapter Thirteen

"Attention, all units! Shots fired! I repeat shots fired on Fairmont and Crotona Avenue!"

When the dispatcher came through the radio, Detective Gonsalez and his partner of ten years, Detective Rosario were on their lunch break. Not wanting to be the last ones to arrive at the scene, they cut their lunch break short and raced toward the scene.

"Unit 3 enroute! I repeat unit 3 enroute!" Detective Rosario said into his walkie-talkie as Detective Gonsalez pushed the pedal on their unmarked car. The two detectives were part of the Homicide Division. In fact, they were the lead detectives.

By the time they made it to the scene, the EMS workers were wheeling a black male into the back of the ambulance. Not too far away, Detective Rosario spotted another body lying on the floor with a white sheet over it.

A few inches away, he also spotted the bullet riddle Nissan Altima. Shaking his head, he made his way over to where Detective Gonsalez stood with the first two officers on the scene.

Chapter Fourteen

"Mmmmm! Oohhh yesss Daadddyyy! Fuck this puss-pussy! I'm-I-I-I'm cumming!" Star moaned as Boo fucked her in the doggy style position, while at the same time he stuck his thumb in and out of her ass taking her to another level.

"Yuh love this dicc right?" Boo asked while he long stroked her nice and slow; and then fast again. *"Yessss Papi! I love thi-thi-this dickkk!"* Star let out another moan as she squirted all over Boo's dick and stomach.

Seeing his dick get coated with Star's cum, he wasn't able to hold back any longer. *"Ahhhhhhh!"* Boo let out a moan of his own; "damn this pussy good ma," he then added while he pulled out of Star's cum-soaked pussy, slapping her on her ass.

Star's real name is Sasha 'Star' Carter. She was half Dominican and half African-American. She stood 5 feet 5 with long yet black hair which stretches to the middle of her back; brown skinned and with a body that females twice her age would die for.

At only 17 years old Star had a lot going on for herself. She lives in the Clinton Towers on Clinton Avenue. Whenever the block was hot, Star's place was where Boo would go until things cooled off.

Boo's trap phone started ringing and he answer on the first ring. *"Yo!"* He said into the receiver. *"Yo Boo, where yuh at? I need to see yuh. I'm out front; I need ten of them thang!"* the voice on the other end shot back.

"Shit, yuh gon need to come down to the Clinton Towers, I'm not at 620 right now; the blocc too hot. Come see me down here, I'm in buildin 740." Boo said. *"Aight, bet I'll be there in five."* The voice on the other end responded before ending the call.

Pookie was one of Boo's favorite customers because whenever he came to see him he always copped ten or better in one shot. *"Where yuh goin babe?"* Star asked as Boo Started getting up off of the bed. *"I'm about to go see this nigga downstairs real quicc. I'm coming right bacc up. I aint goin any where ma. I'm stucc with yuh all day today."* Boo answered as he put on his basketball short and slid on his sneakers without any socks.

After he had finished dressing up, Boo made his way out of Star's apartment to go meet Pookie. Things couldn't have been going any better for Boo. When he first started off, he had started with a few grams of coke. Fast forward to a few months later and now he was running through 100 grams in a matter of five days.

"Pookie wats the word old head?" Boo asked as he opened the building's door to let Pookie inside of the building.

"Aint shit youngen. Yuh kno me, I'm just tryin to get my mind right!" Pookie shot back.

Pookie wore a pair of ripped up, old, dirty pair of Levi jeans; he had no shirt on and on his feet he had on a pair of old dirty white uptowns. The smell of dried piss was oozing through his clothes, causing Boo to frown. He couldn't understand how Pookie always had money to buy drugs, but to fix himself up; he never made the time for that.

Pookie reached in his pocket and came out with a $100 bill in his hand; even the $100 bill was dirty. Boo shook his head but gladly accepted the money. After making sure that the money was in fact a real $100 bill; Boo placed it in his basketball shorts pockets. He then handed Pookie thirteen dimes of crack cocaine.

"Thank yuh youngen." Pookie said. *"Yuh already kno how I do old head, come see me when thats gone,"* Boo responded. *"Put that shit away before yuh walk out this building,"* he added opening the door for Pookie to step out of the building.

81

After Boo had made sure that Pookie was long gone, He made his way back upstairs to finish what him and Star had already started.

- - -

– Meanwhile –

"I'm at the crib, Yuh can pull on me." Legend said into the receiver as he took a few pulls out of the blunt of haze he has been smoking on. Like everyone else, Legend had been laying low as well after the incident in Fairmont Avenue had taken place.

Hughes was so hot that if you didn't know any better, you would have thought the body had dropped in H-Blocc. Legend wasn't tripping though, because no matter how hot the block was, he was still able to get his hustle on.

'Niggas' still needed to get high and he had whatever they wanted. All they had to do was call. The person who Legend was just on the phone with was his plug; his plug had just called him to inform him that he was on his way to come see him. He said that he had some new weed for him to try.

The money was rolling in for Legend and he wouldn't have wanted it any other way; but you know what they say, the more money – the more problems.

Chapter Fifteen

– Two Weeks Later –

It's been four months now since True Blue and Lil Rico returned home; and it's been two weeks since the incident had taken place in Fairmont Avenue. The blue and white had finally stopped circling the block. Little by little, the block was starting to get back to how it used to be before all the chaos broke loose.

Cavs and his flunkies had finally agreed to fall in line. They no longer were free lancing; they were now getting money for True Blue and Lil Rico. True Blue and Lil Rico thought that was the smartest thing they could have done.

One, if they didn't come on board, then they would have had to go out their way to make sure they stood on their word. Secondly, all the unnecessary attention would have had both of the blocks on fire; which would have stopped them from getting any money.

Although the Fairmont niggas were laying low since the incident took place, they knew that it was only a matter of time before they retaliated. Therefore, they decided to stay on point 24/7; getting caught lacking wasn't an option.

The name of the nigga that got shot on his back was Twin. Twin was also a Crip and the other twin was a blood.

The nigga that got killed was Lil Chris, he wasn't from Fairmont, but he was Noni's lil' brother; and that alone made matter that much worst.

Lil Rico's phone rang, he answered on the second ring. *"Yo, west craccin cuhz."* Lil Rico answered, already knowing who was on the other end of the phone. *"Aint shit, coolin at the crib loc. I was callin yuh to let yuh kno that a S600 bike been passin through the clocc nonstop for the last 20mins cuhz. Make sure yall niggas be on point when y'all do decide to cracc out."* Remo said, putting Lil Rico on to game.

"Oh word? Say no more cuhz! Look, do me a favor loco n let me kno when that bike comes bacc around." Lil Rico quickly shot back thinking of the perfect plan. *"Copy, say no more loco."* Remo responded before ending the call.

"Who was that on the jacc loco?" True Blue inquired as he passed Legend the blunt of weed. Legend took a few pulls and then passed it to Lil Rico. With everything that's been going on, Lil Rico had stopped going to parole.

A lot of niggas got caught slipping at parole in the past and he refused to be added to that count. Since Lil Rico now had a parole warrant out for his arrest, he decided to start getting high again. *'Fucc it!'* – that was his attitude.

"That was Remo loco, he said them Fairmont niggas been spinnin the blocc in a S600 for the past 20mins." Lil Rico finally said remembering where he had seen the S600 bike at before. *"Oh word! Say no more then loco, I'm gone take care of that nigga ASAP!"* Legend was the first to say.

Legend had been dying to prove himself to True Blue and Lil Rico; and today was the perfect opportunity he thought. A few minutes passed and the call that Lil Rico was waiting on finally came through.

"Ayo cuhz, that was Remo, he said that the same bike is comin bacc up 179th right now." Lil Rico said, once he had ended the call. Without a second thought, Legend grabbed the 9mm Rugar off the bed. After making sure it was locked and loaded, he snatched his black Nike hoody off of the room's door knob and exited the apartment with True Blue right behind him.

By the time True Blue and Legend reached the corner of 178th street, the S600 was stuck at the light on the corner of East Tremont and Hughes. Throwing his hoody over his head, Legend slowly jogged toward the bike. Once close enough, he raised the 9mm at the back of the biker's head and fired.

BOOM!

BOOM!

The hollow tips penetrated the helmet like it was nothing. Chunks of brain matter and pieces of the helmet were splattered on the back of the window shield of the car that was in front of him. Civilians and innocent bystanders were running and ducking, trying to avoid getting hit by a stray bullet.

Legend wasted no time running up a few more steps, he then fired another six shots hitting the biker all in his upper back and turning his biker jacket into Swiss cheese.

BOOM!

BOOM!

BOOM!

BOOM!

BOOM!

BOOM!

"Bitch ass nigga!" Legend said before taking off running in the opposite direction. True Blue stood on the corner of 178th and Hughes with a smile on his face. He loved how Legend didn't hesitate to put in work. Witnessing that for himself, he learned to respect Legend a lot more then what he already did. Once Legend took off running, True Blue walked inside of Big Homie's store.

- - -

– A Few Days Later –

It's been a few days since the body had dropped on the corner of Hughes Avenue and East Tremont. Although it's been a few days, the block was still somewhat hot with the Police patrolling the area on a regular basis; however, that didn't stop the kids or their parents from enjoying the beautiful summer day.

The pumps were open on H-Blocc with every kid in the neighborhood outside playing and interacting with one another. True Blue was standing with Lil Rico in front of the building 620 on 178th street when his phone started going off in his pockets.

"Yo!" Lil Rico said into the receiver. *"Yo AL where yuh at? I just spoke to Danny n he ask me to call yuh bcos Delanie wants a water gun and he wanted to see if yuh can do me the favor n get her one for me on East Tremont."* Amanda said.

Dannie was day one; he was currently incarcerated and was serving a 2 to 4 years sentence on an assault case. Amanda was the mother of his five years old daughter. *"Oh Amanda wats craccin? Yuh kno that shit aint about nothing loca, give me a minute I'm gon go picc it up now n go over there to drop it off to yuh."* Lil Rico said back. Delanie was not only Dannie's daughter; she was also Lil Rico's god-daughter. *"Okay, thank yuh, yuh kno where we at!"* Amanda replied ending the call.

It took Lil Rico and True Blue no longer than 20 minutes to go and stop on East Tremont to purchase the water gun and afterwards, they made their way toward Mapes Avenue – Amanda's block which was only a few blocks away from Hughes Avenue also Known as 'H-Blocc.'

Making the left onto Mapes Avenue, it wasn't hard to locate Amanda and her friends sitting on the front of her mother's building. All the kids were near the pump, getting wet and having a good time.

"Wats craccin Amanda? I see y'all out here turnin up!" Lil Rico said as he and True Blue reached the front of the building seeing Amanda. *"Yuh kno how we do over here nigga! Ain't shit change!"* Amanda shot back, taking the water gun out of Lil Rico's hands.

"Yeah, yuh kno I kno." Lil Rico responded, already knowing how Amanda and her sisters turn up from experience. *"Whos that nigga yuh came over here with?"* Amanda then asked, pointing in the direction where True Blue was leaning up against a parked car. Lil Rico turned around to see who she was referring to.

"Oh, that's my brother 'A' he just came home last week." Lil Rico responded nonchalantly. *"Oh word! That*

nigga looks gooooddd!" Amanda finally said, dragging the word 'good' for emphasis. Lil Rico just shook his head without any further comment on the subject.

"Look, make sure yuh let Delanie kno I got her water gun. I would have gone over n said hi to her, but it looks like she's havin too much of a good time n I don't want to intervene." Lil Rico said. *"Okay, thank yuh once again Al."* Amanda shot back. After they said their goodbyes, Lil Rico and True Blue started to make their way off the block.

- - -

"Damn Amanda, who the hell was that nigga that came over here with Al?" Nieves – a family friend said as soon as Lil Rico and True Blue were out of sight. *"That nigga looks good!"* she then added.

"Yeah, he deff is a cutie, if I wasn't taken, I would have deff been tryin to holla!" Eileen, one of Amanda's older sister added. *"Yeah, that nigga looks good enough to eat! He can deff get it!"* Aisha, Amanda's other sister finally said and they all laughed.

"Oh shit, look at y'all bitches! Mad thirsty! And look at yuh, since when yuh talk like that?" Amanda asked, focusing her attention on Aisha. *"I bet that nigga got that*

celibate pussy nice and moist huh?" She added and once again, they all burst into laughter.

Chapter Sixteen

Aisha was 5 feet 9, 150lbs, light skinned with long black hair stretching to the middle of her back; with a nice round ass, not too big and not to small, which was just right for her body. Her beautiful face was the icing on the cake. The frames she wore gave her that school teacher kind of look. Her sex appeal was through the roof.

Since the first day that True Blue had laid his eyes on Aisha he couldn't seem to get her out of his mind. She was all he thought about even though he didn't even really know her; but for some reason, he felt like he knew her. Aisha was his type and he knew a keeper when he saw one. He definitely wanted to make Aisha his woman. In his mind, Aisha was already his and she doesn't even know it.

After dropping the water gun off to Amanda, True Blue and Lil Rico ended up going back to Mapes two more times. At first True Blue wasn't trying to do all the back forth but after laying his eyes on Aisha he didn't mind the going back and forth to Mapes; as long as he got a chance see his soon to be wife again.

On the second trip to Mapes, OT had given Lil Rico and True Blue a ride since he was on H-Blocc at the time. *"Yo, OT! Hold up! Hold up!"* True Blue said, causing OT to step on the breaks quite suddenly. *"Fuck wrong with yuh nigga?"* OT shot back but got no response. Turning towards the back seat all he could see was True Blue's back, as he already jumped out of the truck.

Coming down the block on the opposite street was Aisha. *"Hey wats sup beautiful?"* True Blue said once he was inches away from Aisha. *"My name is Andy, but my friends call me 'A',"* he added extended his hands for a hand shake.

Aisha looked at him surprised by his actions. She couldn't believe that the same nigga that she couldn't get her mind off was standing right in front of her; looking even better close and personal.

"Hey, I'm Aisha; Nice to meet yuh." Aisha responded, shaking True Blue's hands. *"Listen ma, I'm kind of in a rush right now n it seem like yuh was on ya way to rejoin ya sisters n friends. I'm not tryin to hold yuh up, so if it's oKay with yuh. I would love for us to exchange numbers. There's something about yuh that has me intrigued."* True Blue said smoothly licking his bottom lip; causing Aisha to switch from one leg to the other.

That was almost three weeks ago; and ever since True Blue and Aisha had exchanged numbers, they haven't stopped calling or testing each other. They were enjoying each other's company more and more as the time went on.

Before they knew it, Mapes became True Blue and Lil Rico's second block. Whenever H-Blocc got hot, Mapes was the place to be until things cooled off.

In the short month that True Blue had gotten to know Aisha, he learned that she had a eight years old daughter whose name was Hailey, she was twenty eight years old, had her own apartment in the Courtland section of the Bronx; and that she worked as a Registered Nurse for a private clinic.

True Blue also learned that she had been celibate for almost two years. Aisha was every letter of the word independent; which is one thing True Blue loved about her, because he too was one. Aisha was the total package.

Although it's been almost a month that they had started talking, True Blue and Aisha still haven't had any sex. True Blue wasn't tripping though. He was on her time not his; he wasn't trying to rush anything with her; he knew that when the time was right, they would cross that bridge.

- - -

H-Blocc had been on fire for the past three days, due to all the gun violence and drug dealing that was taking place there. Due to that fact alone, True Blue, Boo, Legend and Lil Rico were on Mapes Avenue chilling, drinking, smoking and enjoying the nice summer weather.

94

Their little party always lasted till the next day and today wasn't any different. Normally, when the sun would start to rise, True Blue and his squad would say their goodbyes, but on this particular morning Aisha had asked True Blue to stay behind with her.

They were both feeling real nice and had spent most of the night making out n fondling each other. It was safe to say that they were both horny and ready to take the next step in their relationship.

Soon after Lil Rico, Boo and Legend left of the block, Aisha and True Blue decided to take the after party into Aisha's mother's house. Although she had her own apartment, Aisha still had her own room in her mother's apartment.

Just right after they both entered her room, they started ripping each other's clothes of their bodies. True Blue pinned Aisha against the wall and started kissing and licking her on her neck. *"Ohhh! That feelllls gooood papi!"* Aisha moaned into True Blue's ears.

After they were both in their birthday suits, True Blue led Aisha toward the king size bed that sat on the corner of the room. Laying her on her back, True Blue spread her legs with his fingers and started playing in her wet pussy.

95

"Ohhhh my gud!" Aisha let out another moan. Loving the way True Blue's fingers felt on her clit. Taking his fingers out of Aisha's pussy, he took them straight to his mouth. Loving the way Aisha tasted, he decided to replace his fingers with his mouth.

True Blue ate on Aisha's pussy as if it was the last supper. He didn't stop until she had two back to back orgasms in his mouth. Satisfied with his work, he got up and turned Aisha in the doggie style position.

Once positioned behind her, he slowly entered her tight wet pussy. *"Yesss daadddddy, fuccckk thisss pussy."* Aisha said in between moans. Her pussy was so tight and wet that True Blue was almost close to cumming after only being inside of her for two seconds.

"Damn ma, this pussi feels sooo good." True Blue said out of breath. Yes the pussy was that good. True Blue and Aisha ended up fucking each other until they both ended up having explosive orgasm.

They couldn't get enough of one another. They loved the way their body felt against each other. True Blue loved the way her pussy wrapped around his dick and Aisha love the way his dick felt inside of her. Before they knew it, they both drifted off into a deep sleep. The Henny, weed, smoke and the two hours of steamy sex had them both exhausted and drained.

Chapter Seventeen

"Can yuh fuckin believe that it's almost been three weeks and we still don't even have the smallest lead on this fuckin case?" Detective Rosario asked his partner Detective Gonsalez as they cruised the streets of the South Bronx.

"Yeah, tell me about it. Everybody stickin to the so called code of the streets; but I tell yuh one thing, we gon get those sons of a bitch one way or another! Believe that!" Detective Gonsalez shot back meaning every word he had spoken.

When the incident on Fairmont and Crotona Avenues first happened, the two detectives where on a mission to try to get any video surveillance in hope to catch the shooter or the shooters; but the search was to no avail.

The cameras weren't showing any sign of the shooter or shooters; the only thing that could be seen on the footage was the flash of the gun every time that it went off. Their higher ups were on the line and solving this case could maybe save their careers and job.

"I dont give a damn! Watever yuh guys have to do to solve this fuckin case better be done! The fuckin higher ups are on my line n i dont fuckin like it, not one bit! Dont come back to my fuckin office without the fuckin shooter in custody!" The last conversation Detective Gonsalez had with

his Captain played over and over in his head. He knew that Captain Tavera wasn't playing and meant every word he had spoken.

Their only luck at getting the shooter off the streets went out the window when they went to pay a visit to Jonathan Mendez, a.k.a. Twin at the hospital he was being treated. Twin denied seeing or knowing the shooter and thus cutting their chances of catching the shooter or the shooters from nine out of ten to one in a million; and that alone didn't sit well with the Detectives.

Jorge Gonsalez is 53 years old and has been part of the NYPD for the past twenty years. He stood 5 feet 9, 198 lbs, brown skin complexion, with salt and pepper hair which he always kept low in a ceaser style. Detective Gonsalez was assigned to the Homicide Division.

Tone Rosario has been in the force for 15 years and out of the 15 years, he had spent the last 10 years as Detective Gonsalez's partner. They were like Batman and Robbin in the streets of NY. Standing at 5 feet 11, 220 lbs, low ceaser haircut, brown skin, with the left arm covered in a trivial tattoo all the way up to his shoulders; Detective Rosario was in his late 30s.

- - -

– Meanwhile ... –

Aisha couldn't seem to get her mind off of True Blue. There wasn't a minute out of her day that she didn't think about him or have him in mind. To her, True Blue was the total package.

Standing at 5 feet 10, caramel skin complexion, low ceaser cut with 360 waves through his whole head; so handsome that rating him from a 1 to 10, to her he rates 11. Tattoos cover his body and his 'street status' screamed 'Boss!'

Aisha normally stayed at her mother's house, but today was different. She and True Blue had plans to meet up at her apartment when the sun went down; so, staying in her mother's house was out of the equation tonight.

"Hailey can yuh hurry up? The cab should be here in another two mins." Aisha shouted into the back room where Hailey was getting all her stuff together. *"I'm ready mom,"* Hailey came out of the back room saying, with her Book bag hanging off her shoulders.

Hailey never liked any of the men her mother had dated before, but for some reason she liked to see her mom with True Blue. When her mom was around True Blue, she

100

could see it in her mom's face that she was happy. On top of all of that, True Blue treated her mom like a queen.

Aisha loves the bond that True Blue and Hailey have been building in the past two months; to her surprise, Hailey and True Blue got alone pretty good and she wouldn't have wanted it any other way.

"Okay come Boo-Boo, the cab should be outside." Aisha finally said calling Hailey by the nick name she had given her when she was first born.

- - -

– On the Other Side –

The block has been jumping with activities for the past three days. The heat had finally started to die down which was a good thing for the business. It was only 11.00am and True Blue had already run through 7 bundles of the checker board. The fiends loved the work and as long as they came correct, True Blue and Lil Rico were going to make sure that they got whatever they had come for.

On this beautiful Saturday morning, True Blue, Legend, Lil Rico and Boo sat outside of Big Homie Deli's grocery store enjoying the weather, smoking and getting rid of their drugs of choice.

Big Homie was now part of the team; when the situation took place with Legend, Big Homie had deleted any footage of the shooting before the Police even showed up to the scene. With that alone he earned their respect, love and loyalty.

"Wat y'all niggas fuccin wit today?" Boo asked no one in particular. *"Shit nigga, I'm on the blocc all day today until the Police come!"* Lil Rico quickly shot back taking a pull out of the blunt of weed he been smoking on.

"Yeah, I'm here wit the cuhz, yuh kno we cant leave him out here dolo" Legend added, sealing close the blunt he had just finished rolling. *"Nigga, I aint stayin on this hot ass blocc today. I have a date with my baby tonight!"* True Blue finally said getting up from the milk crate he had been sitting on.

After serving the fiend, True Blue sat back down on the milk crate and took the blunt that Lil Rico was offering him. Immediately it hit 8.00pm, True Blue decided to go and get ready for his date.

The sun was now beginning to set on his way into Legend's apartment he reached in his pockets for his phone and sent Aisha a text which read: *'Hey sexy, I'm about to get in the shower now. When yuh see this message, send me ya addy mami. I cant wait to spend time wit yuh n lil l <3'*

After sending the message, he undressed and jumped straight in the shower. Fifteen minutes later, he was out of the shower and dressed to impress in his all black and green Gucci outfit with the matching low top Gucci sneakers to match.

Walking into Legend's room, he noticed that the three of them were in there smoking and playing 2k on the PS4. *"Ayo, I'm about to dip; make sure y'all hit my line if anything, csafe!"* True Blue said to his men before walking out of the apartment.

Being that he still had the rental that he and his lil homie, Nito had rented, he didn't have to worry about how he was going to get to Aisha's house. After he got behind the steering wheels of the silver 2015 Toyota Camry, he pulled out of the parking space and made his way toward his future wife's apartment.

Chapter Eighteen

Legend was sitting in his room when his trap phone started going off on the bed. Getting up from the small couch, he walked over to the bed and picked up the call before it was sent to voice mail.

"Yo! Wats the word?" Legend said into the receiver. *"Hey Legend it's me Stephanie from 179th, I was callin to see if yuh was around. I need to see yuh. I'm inside of Big Homies store."* Stephanie responded.

"Oh, hey wats sup ma. And for yuh I'm gon always be around ma. All yuh have to do is call n I'll pop up." Legend said back smoothly, causing Stephanie to blush on the other end of the phone. Legend has been trying to get Stephanie since the first day they met on East Tremont, but she was always playing hard to get.

"Oh okay, cool! I need two 8ths of that new grand daddy kush yuh got. I'm gon meet yuh here in the store." Stephanie finally said after she got herself together. *"Copy! Say no more, I'll be right there sexy."* Legend responded.

After he ended the call, he went into his stash of weed and grabbed the two 8ths of grand daddy kush for Stephanie. Before leaving the apartment, he grabbed his .357 and placed it by his hip.

"Hey watssup sexy!" Legend said walking into the store. He embraced her into a hug and in one motion he dropped the two 8ths in her grocery bag. *"Wats craccin Big Homie,"* he added.

"Hey yuh! Thank yuh for meetin me here. I'm kind of in a rush, if not I would stopped by ya crib." Stephanie explained handing Legend a $50 bill for the two 8ths. After she paid for her grocery, they both walked out of the store.

"So, wat yuh about to get into? I kno yuh aint about to smoke those two 8ths by ya'self!" Legend asked when they came to a stop on the corner of 178th and Hughes Avenue. *"Oh no, yuh no I aint that much of a smoker; I'm just buyin this for my next door neighbor, she givin me two dimes for gettin it for her."* Stephanie shot back.

Legend couldn't stop staring at how sexy Stephanie was looking in her all blue leggings with the matching all black and blue Jordon 1s. Stephanie was Puerto Rican and black; she favors the actress Jessica Alba.

"Copy, so when yuh gon stop frontin n let a nigga light yuh up one of these days?" Legend said changing the subject. Stephanie didn't reply right away; her attention was on the two hooded men that were making their way up the block. She couldn't understand how niggas were wearing hoodies in the middle of July.

Seeing the way she was looking behind him, Legend then turned his attention in the same direction Stephanie was looking at, but by that time, the two hooded niggas were only ten feet away from them with their guns in hands aiming at Legend's direction.

BOOM!

BOOM!

BOOM!

BOC!

BOC!

As the first shot went off, Legend tried to push Stephanie out of harm's way while at the same time he dove behind the parked car that was sitting idle on the corner of 178th.

BOC!

BOC!

BOOM!

Legend heard three more shots go off; by now, he had his .357 in hand waiting on the perfect time to return fire. He knew who the two gunmen were; and that they meant business from the choice of power they brought with them.

Getting a squad position, Legend let off two shots in the direction where he had last seen the shooters standing at;

his plan wasn't to hit anyone of them, but more importantly he was trying to make sure they didn't try to box him in.

They exchanged fire for what seem like two hours but it was only two minutes; the car Legend was hiding behind of looked like Swiss cheese as it rocked back and forth every time a slug penetrated and hit a part of it.

The sound of the Police siren were getting louder which only meant they were getting closer by the minute. To avoid being caught at the scene, the two shooters raced off the scene before it was too late.

When Legend felt like the coast was clear, he got up from behind the car; examining the car he said to himself, *"Damn, these niggas ain't come to play."* as he saw the car that saved his life looking like a slice of Swiss cheese.

He finally remembered Stephanie and made his way around the corner. *"Damn! fucc!"* he cursed out loud as he spotted Stephanie's body lying in a pool of her own blood; with two shots in her face and one in the middle of her chest. Seeing that there was nothing that he could have done for her, he ran off the scene into his building 620.

- - -

Meanwhile, Lil Rico and Flaca had just finished another round of some hot steamy sex when they heard the first three shots go off. The shots sounded so close that if you ain't know any better you would have thought they were fired inside of the building and not up the block.

"Oh shit!" Lil Rico said jumping off the bed remembering that he had left Legend on the block. Getting up off the bed, he picked up his basketball shorts off the floor. Just as he took his phone out of his pockets, it started ringing in his hands; looking at the caller ID, it read 'Legend' on the screen.

"Yo, cuhz wat the fucc goin on out there! Yuh good?" Lil Rico asked with concern though happy to hear his man's voice on the other end of the phone. *"Yeah, I'm gucci loco, but them niggas just came sliding through tryin to catch a nigga laccin. Where yuh at?"* Legend said.

"I'm down the blocc, in Flaca's crib." Lil Rico answered as he quickly got dressed. *"Oh, aight copy! Pull up to my shit asap; but leave the strap in Flaca's crib; them boys in blue there heavy,"* Legend said before he ended the call.

When Lil Rico got off the phone, he looked over at Flaca who was now in sitting position on the bed with a concerned look on her face. *"Listen ma, everything is fine; don't worry about nothin okay?"* Lil Rico said. Flaca just shook her head up and down.

"I'm gon slide out of here, but I need to leave my gun here for now. I'll be bacc to get it before the night is over." Lil Rico then added. *"Tabien papi,"* Flaca shot back in Spanish without saying another word; Lil Rico threw his shirt over his head and made his way out of Flaca's room and apartment.

Flaca's real was Yukersie Domingo; she is a full blown Dominican standing at 5 feet 6, 140 lbs and thick in all the right places with long brown hair which extends to the middle of her back. Flaca is 22 and only spoke enough English to get by.

Lil Rico made it up the block and was happy that he had listened to Legend and didn't bring his pistol with him. The cops and the crime scene team were all over the place searching for any evidence and snapping pictures of Stephanie's corpse on the floor.

"Damn Steph." Lil Rico thought to himself recognizing Stephanie on sight. The two of them had attended the same school back in the days and were even seeing each other at some point. Lil Rico made it into 620 without any of the Police officers on the scene harassing him.

"Yo wat the fucc happened out there cuhz?" Lil Rico asked Legend as soon as he entered the apartment. He was still a little fucked up about seeing Stephanie sprawled out on

the floor dead. *"Them niggas killed Steph; and she aint even have shit to do wit this shit,"* he added, taking a seat on Legend's bed.

"Yeah I kno crody, shit sad; me n her was choppin it up when all the shit went down. It's sad that she got caught in the cross fire." Legend said shaking his head from side to side.

"Wats up with True Blue, he kno yet?" Lil Rico asked. *"He still over at Aisha's crib. I tried callin him a few times but he ain't answer any of my calls."* Legend responded as he lit the blunt he had just finished rolling, trying to get his nerves under control.

Legend and Lil Rico decided to play the crib for the rest of the night, until they figured out what was it that they were going to do. One thing for sure and two thing certain; they weren't going to be able to get any money on the block for a little while especially since an innocent bystander got caught in the cross fire. That was bad for business.

Chapter Nineteen

Detective Gonsalez and Detective Rosario were getting into their unmarked car in the 48th precinct parking lot when the dispatchers came through the radio. *"Attention all units! Attention all units! Shots fired on 178th and Hughes! I repeat shots fired!"*

The two detectives wasted no time getting into their squad car and racing toward the scene. The only thing they were hoping for was that there wasn't a body on the ground and if there was, that they at least have a lead on the suspect or suspects.

It took the two detectives 5 minutes in total to get to the scene on 178th and Hughes avenue; when they arrived on the scene, the first thing they spotted was the crime scene unit putting the white sheet over a dead body on the ground, while the others snapped pictures of the scene. *"This can't be good,"* Detective Gonsalez said as he parked the car and jumped out.

"What do we have here?" Detective Gonsalez asked the crime scene Police officer. *"A female, looks to be about 20 to 23 years old. She was shot three times. Once in the chest and twice in the face,"* the crime scene officer stated as he continued to take pictures of the scene.

111

Detective Rosario was also speaking to the first unit on the scene. *"When we got here, everything was how yuh see it now. No one is claimin to see anything,"* the officer in blue said. Detective Rosario hissed in disappointment.

"Did yuh guys check on the cameras in the store yet?" Detective Rosario asked. *"No detective, we was waitin on y'all arrival, before we did anything,"* the officer in blue quickly shot back. *"Okay, thanks and good job!"* Detective Rosario said before walking off in the direction Detective Gonsalez was standing.

The two detectives then started making their way into the store, hoping that the store's cameras had caught the shooting on footage. Five minutes later Detective Gonsalez and Detective Rosario walked out of Big Homie's store pissed the hell off. Once again, Big Homie had come through.

"The Feds is gon definitely be all over this. It's been three bodies in a matter of weeks; and we still don't have the smallest clue on either one of them," Detective Gonsalez said shaking his head and fearing the worst. *"Yeah, tell me about it, we might not even have a job when it's all said n done with,"* Detective Rosario added in disbelief.

Chapter Twenty

"Ayo, yuh seen that nigga's face when he turned around to see us?" Noni asked taking a pull out of the blunt he and June had been smoking. *"Yeah scrap, them shits got bigger than a soccer ball!"* June responded *"that's fucked up that shorty got caught up in the middle of the shit tho,"* he then added taking the blunt out of Noni's hand.

"Nigga, fuck that bitch n them bitch ass Hughes niggas. If yuh wit them niggas, then yuh gon get it the same way they gon get it every time!" Noni quickly shot back, not really feeling June's last comment. June decided to let the conversation die and continued smoking on the blunt of haze.

Jason 'Noni' Perez was 23 years old. Born in Puerto Rico and raised in the United States; his parents migrated from PR when he was just 5 years old. Noni stood 5 feet 6, 165lbs with a light brown skin, low ceaser haircut and with a few tattoos covering his arms and chest.

Noni has a short temper; and after losing his parent to a drug over doze, his temper issue only got worse. Lil Chris was the only thing he had left in this word: and now that he was gone, he really felt like he has nothing to live for anymore. Noni barely did any talking, he loved letting his gun do all the talking for him at all times.

113

Junior 'June' Lopez was 22 years old and his parents were natives of the Dominican Republic. Unlike Noni, June was born in the United States. Growing up, June was never in want of anything; his parents always made sure that he had everything he needed or wanted.

However, unlike Noni, June had chosen the streets. June stood at 6 feet 2, 175lbs with a skin complexion the color of a paper bag; his low ceaser haircut had some thick waves. June too loved to let his gun do all the talking for him.

Noni and June had the Fairmont and Crotona section of the Bronx in frenzy; nothing went down or moved unless they 'okayed' it. Noni's phone started ringing and he answered it on the second ring.

"Yo! Wats poppin?" Noni said into the receiver. *"Yo wats craccin loco, wat y'all niggas fuccin with?"* The voice on the other end of the phone shot back. *"Aint shit scrap, coolin in the spot, the block too hot right now for niggas to be out there lookin like sittin ducks, feel me?"* Noni retorted, lighting the fresh rolled blunt he had just finish rolling while on the phone.

"Tell me about it, I already know I'm about to come through tho; make sure y'all open the door for me." The

voice on the other end said. *"Nigga pull up, yuh kno where we at!"* Noni stated before ending the call.

"Nigga who the hell yuh tellin our location too?" June asked concern. *"Nigga calm the fuck down, that wasn't nobody but Trey! With ya scary ass!"* Noni shot back with a frown on his face.

- - -

– Meanwhile … –

"Ayo cuz I'm about to slide up out of here, I got a move to make." Trey said stepping back into Legend's room; Legend, Boo and Lil Rico were all there in Legend's room. The four of them had been kicking it while smoking on a few blunts of grand daddy kush, for the past two hours. *"Y'all niggas csafe out here."* Trey added, giving all three of them some dap before walking out of the room and out of the apartment.

"I ain't gon lie, I kno thats y'all loc, but I dont trust that nigga. Something aint right wit that nigga." Legend was the first to say as soon as Trey was out of sight. *"Nah cuhz, yuh trippin. Trey good money cuhz, he's one of the day one loco."* Boo quickly retorted in Trey's defence.

"Yeah, I hear yuh, but my gut feelin never wrong. I'm gon keep my eyes on tha nigga still loco," Legend shot back sticking to his guns. After their little conversation about

115

Trey, the three of them continued to smoke and play the PS4 while they got money and served every fiend that called their trap phone.

Chapter Twenty-One

Today, work wasn't as busy as it used to be normally for Aisha and she was thankful for that. Last night was long night for her; she couldn't seem to be able to get True Blue out of her mind ever since she got to her job. *"Damn that nigga got me fallin for his ass."* Aisha thought to herself.

Another thing that had her nervous was that her period was two weeks late and that could have only meant one thing: she was pregnant. As much as she didn't want to be pregnant, she knew that it was a strong possibility that she was; being that she and True Blue never bothered to use protection when they had sex.

It was 11.00am and being that she doesn't have much to do, she decided to go meet up with her sister Eileen so both of them can go get some lunch together. *"Hey watssup! How is work goin for yuh today?"* Aisha asked her sister Eileen as they were walking to the pizza shop on east Tremont Avenue.

"Work is stressful for me today. It seem like every time I get done with a pile of papers, these niggas comes n drop off another stack." Eileen said, referring to their boss. *"Well, too, bad I can't say the same. Work been pretty easy for me today, n in a way I like it like that b cos I'm tired; me*

n True Blue didn't go to sleep till 4.00am this morning." Aisha stated as they entered the pizza shop.

While in the pizza shop, they walked towards the back and took a seat on one of the tables facing the window; not too long after, the waiter came and took their orders. They both ordered a slice of pizza with extra cheese with a Pepsi soda to wash it down with.

"Wats wrong with yuh? Yuh look like somethin is weighing heavy on ya mind?" Eileen asked seeing the look on her sister's face. *"I'm two weeks late,"* Aisha finally said after a few minutes had gone by, not really trying to make eye contact with her sister.

"OMG! I'm about to be a aunty again!" Eileen shouted a little too loud for Aisha. *"Whose is it? True's?"* Eileen questioned Aisha. *"If I am, then yes, It's True's. I wasn't fuckin anybody for almost two years until I met True n he's the only one I been sleepin with."* Aisha said with a concerned look on her face. *"I don't know if I'm ready for another child,"* she added.

"If yuh are tho, an abortion is out of the equation!" Eileen said firmly. "I think we should stop at the pharmacy and get you at least two or three pregnancy test kit on our way back to work to make sure," she stated further.

118

After the two sisters finished their lunch, they both made their way to the pharmacy to buy the three pregnancy test kit; 45 minutes later, Aisha came out of the bathroom with her eyes puffy from the crying she had been doing for the past ten minutes: she was pregnant with True Blue's child.

Walking into her office, Aisha picked up her phone from her desk and decided to send True Blue a text stating: *"Babe, when yuh get the chance or when I come home later, we need to talk."* After rereading the message, Aisha pressed 'send' on her phone and afterwards, she placed the phone back on her desk and walked out of her office to go tell her sister the good news.

Aisha walked into Eileen's office and saw that her sister was in fact very busy at work. Eileen looked up at her sister for a few seconds before focusing her attention back on the pile of papers on her desk.

"Hey yuh!" Eileen said without looking in Aisha's direction. *"I'm pregnant Eileen,"* Aisha said almost in a whisper. Hearing what her sister had just said caused Eileen to stop what she was doing.

"Forreal!" Eileen said excited for her sister. *"Did yuh tell True yet?"* she added in one breath. *"No not yet, but*

I will once I get out of work n see him later." Aisha said, not knowing how to feel about her new found news.

"Look Aisha, we gon get through this together. I'm gon have ya back every step of the way. Whatever yuh need me to do just say it n I got yuh. Yuh my sister n that's wat sisters are for." Eileen said seeing the look of worry on Aisha's face.

Getting up from her desk, Eileen made her way over to where Aisha was standing and embraced her into a hug and immediately Aisha broke down crying on Eileen's shoulders. *"Thank yuh so much Eileen, I really appreciate yuh be in here for me. Thank yuh for makin me feel a lot better about this situation I found myself,"* Aisha said in between sobs.

Aisha and Eileen talked for a few minutes more; after Aisha got herself together, she left Eileen's office feeling a lot better about her situation. When she got back in her office, Aisha smiled to herself as she rubbed on her own belly and saying to herself: *"We gon get through this together lil one."*

Chapter Twenty-Two

True Blue woke up the next morning and noticed that he was the only one on the bed. *"Damn she left n I ain't even feel her leave,"* he thought to himself as he rolled out of the bed. Walking over to the dresser where his phone was charging, he picked it up and saw that he had 20 missed calls and 10 new messages.

"Damn, who the hell blowin my line up like this?" True Blue said out loud while looking through his call log. Seeing that the majority of the phone calls came from Lil Rico and Legend, he knew that something had to be wrong.

When True Blue read the messages that Legend and Lil Rico had sent him, he knew for sure that something in fact was wrong. Seeing a message from Aisha, he smiled and opened the message. *"We need to talk babe."* was all the message Aisha had sent said.

When he had replied to Aisha's message, he placed the phone back on its charger; before he was able to walk out of the room, the phone started going off with an incoming call. Looking at the caller ID, he answered the call.

"Yo Tsunami, klok my brother?" True Blue said into the receiver. *"Nah aqui chillin, klok yall niggas ready for tonight?"* Tsunami asked, getting straight to the point.

Tsunami was True Blue's childhood friend. They both came up together in the mean streets of the Bronx.

Also, they both attended the same schools, from middle school to high school. A few days prior, Tsunami had informed True Blue about a lick that he had lined up. The lick alone was supposed to be worth $65,000 in cash and five bricks of some white china. In return, Tsunami wanted nothing; all he really cared for was the message that was being sent.

"Oh shit I aint gone lie loco, I forgot; but that shit aint about nothin. Yuh kno we live for shit like this!" True Blue shot back quickly. *"After we get off the phone, I'm gon call Lil Rico n them to let them kno that we movin today,"* he added.

"Tato dale loco, I'll see yuh tonight my guy, love yuh." Tsunami stated before they ended the call. As soon as the call ended, True Blue decided to place a call to Lil Rico. Lil Rico answered on the first ring.

"Damn nigga, Aisha must to have put that pussy on yuh last night. Niggas been blowin up ya phone all mornin." Lil Rico said. *"Yeah, I kno, that's why I'm callin to see why y'all niggas blowin up my phone like y'all niggas don't got no sense!"* True Blue shot back as he walked into the bathroom to ease his bladder.

122

Without leaving anything out, Lil Rico went on to explain everything that had took place with Legend and the opps. *"Damn,"* True Blue said after hearing what had happened to Stephanie. *"Watssup with Legend, yuh sure he good?"* he then asked, concerned.

"Yeah, the cuhz gucci, it was just shorty that got hit." Lil Rico assured him. *"Aight, copy loco, I'm about to hop in the shower right now. I'll see y'all on the blocc."* True Blue said before ending the call.

When he had gotten off the phone with Lil Rico, True Blue sent Reddot a text. Walking into the kitchen, he noticed that there was a note stuck to the refrigerator's door. Taking the note off the fridge, he began to read it.

"Hey handsome! I hope that yuh had a great night sleep <3 Also, I want to thank yuh for such an amazin night! I'm sorry I didn't let yuh kno I was leavin, but yuh was lookin too peaceful sleepin that I didn't want to wake yuh: I kno that yuh may want to shower, the towels are in the closet in the hall way as well as the wash clothes. I can't wait to see yuh again later on tonigh <3"

After reading the note Aisha had left him, True Blue couldn't stop the smile from escaping his lips. That note alone made his feeling for Aisha grow even more than it already was; placing the piece of paper on top of the counter, he made his way over toward the hall way's closet to grab a towel and a wash clothe. Getting in the bathroom, he removed his Ethika boxers and jumped in the shower.

- - -

– Castle Hill, The BX –

Lance 'Reddot' Thomas had just finished getting his early morning nut off. He and his girlfriend, Diamond had been going at it since 7:30am and it was now 11.00am; they couldn't seem to get enough of one another. While they were lying on the bed smoking a fresh rolled blunt, Reddot's phone buzzed, indicating that he had a new message.

"Ma, can yuh pass me my phone." Reddot asked Diamond who was a lot closer than he was to it. Grabbing the phone off the night stand, Diamond handed it over to Reddot. Seeing that new message that came in was from True Blue, he wasted no time in opening it.

"Yo cuhz, get ya ass up, I'm comin to picc yuh up. It's game time!" the text True Blue had sent read. A smile spread across Reddot's face as the thought of putting in work invaded his brain. Rolling out of the bed, he started to make his way out of the room in the direction of the bathroom.

"Babe, yuh dont want this?" Diamond asked referring to the blunt they had been smoking on. *"Nah*

babygirl, thats yuh, I'm gon hop in the shower real quicc; this nigga True on his way over to come get me." Reddot quickly said without turning around to face her. Stepping in the bathroom, Reddot turned the water on in the shower and hopped in.

- - -

As soon as True Blue finished taking a shower, he stepped out of the bathroom and made his way back into Aisha's room. Seeing that the blue light was blinking on and off on his phone, he walked over to the dresser and picked the phone up. Noticing that he had a new message from Aisha, he opened it and began reading it.

"Hey pa, I hope that by the time yuh see this message, that yuh had already showered and made yourself something to eat. Anyways, let me get back to the real reason as why I wrote yuh in the first place. I dont kno how else to say it, so I'm just gon say it... I'm pregnant True."

After reading Aisha's text, True Blue couldn't believe what he had just read. He was happy and worried at the same time. He'd always craved and wanted to have a child, but now that there was a possibility that he might be a father; the thought was over whelming to him.

"Dont worry about it ma, we gon figured this out. Watever yuh decide to do, I'm with yuh 100%. We would talk about this later on. Love yuh" He pressed 'send' on his phone and began to get dressed while the thought of being a father put a smile on his face.

About 15 minutes later, True Blue was pulling up to the Castle Hill Projects in the Bronx. After parking, he took out his phone and gave Reddot a call. *"Yo loco, I'm out front, hurry ya ass up,"* True Blue said into the receiver when Reddot answered.

"Copy loco, I'll be right out," Reddot responded before ending the call. A few seconds passed before Reddot finally came out of the building 545. Walking over to where True Blue was parked in his all black Nike tech suit, he hopped in the Camry.

"Wats craccin cuhz?" Reddot said as soon as he settled into the passenger seat. *"Yuh kno me, yuh never them."* True Blue stated as he pulled the car back into traffic. Coming to a stop at the red light, True Blue lit the half of blunt he had sitting on the ash tray. 'Computers' by 'Rowdy Rebel' thumped out of the car's speakers.

"Watssup cuhz, yuh seem to be in heavy thoughts; yuh good?" Reddot asked turning the music down, sensing that something was wrong with his man. *"Yeah cuhz, I'm*

126

gucci. Aisha text me this mornin about she was pregnant." True Blue stated as he navigated the Camry into the Cross Bronx express way.

"Damn," was all Reddot said; he thought about saying more, but decided to let his man get his thoughts together. Some 20 minutes later, True Blue and Reddot were pulling into a parking space in front of JC's barbershop on Belmont Avenue.

"Yo Cavs, I'm out front, try to hurry up loco I have moves to make." True Blue said into the receiver. *"Copy yai, I'll be down there in two."* Cavs quickly said. *"Copy loco, I'm in front of JC's shop."* True Blue said ending the call.

It took no longer than the 2 minutes that Cavs said he would be walking out of his building before he made his way down to where True Blue was parked. Opening the back door, he jumped in to the car.

"True Blue klok." Cavs said while handing True Blue the brown bag with the week's money in it. Cavs ain't say a word to Reddot, he still felt salty about Reddot shooting him on his knees. Thanks to Reddot he now walked with a permanent limp; something that he wasn't too happy about.

They made the transaction and True Blue let Cavs know that from now on, he would have to see Reddot for his work. Cavs wasn't too cool with the idea, but he was in no position to do or say otherwise. Once the business at hand was concluded, Cavs jumped out of the car; and in no time, True Blue pulled out of the parking space.

- - -

"Yo, I'm not gon lie, I fuckin hate that nigga Reddot Tri-bu!" Cavs said to C-Lite when he got back inside of the apartment they trapped out off. *"Man, fuck that nigga Tri-bu is not even for all of that."* C-Lite shot back not trying to feed into what Cavs was talking about.

The truth of the matter was that C-Lite already had seen Reddot in action a few times and he didn't want to get caught up on no bullshit with him to avoid getting shot or killed. *"Nigga, fuck yuh mean? That nigga shot me, got me walkin with a fuccn limp n yuh over here talkin about that shit ain't for all that! Yuh got me fucked up nigga!"* Cavs said heated by C-Lite's last comment. *"That nigga gon get his, even if that's the last thing I do!"* he added, while a wicked smile spread across his face.

Chapter Twenty-Three

It was 10.00pm on the dot. Lil Rico, Boo, Legend, Reddot and True Blue sat parked across the street from the building they were striking. It was completely silence in the Toyota Camry rental as they waited on the perfect time to make their move.

Everyone in the car was in their own thoughts. *"Click! Clock!"* was all that could be heard in the car as everyone in attendance loaded a live round into their weapons. The building they were striking was located in the under cliff section of the Bronx, by University Avenue.

It was 10:45pm when they all exited the car and made their way into the building unnoticed. The block was empty due to how late it was; the weather was nice, not too hot and not too cold.

When they got inside the building, they made their way up to the fourth floor; locating apartment 4H at the end of the hallway. Only three of them made their way towards their target apartment while Legend and Boo stood back as the look outs.

"Y'all ready?" True Blue asked; and Reddot and Lil Rico nodded their heads up and down. On cue, True Blue started knocking on the door. 'Knock! Knock! Knock!'

giving the door the special knock that Tsunami had told them to use.

A few second after the knock, someone was heard approaching the front door. *"Quienes?"* A Spanish female voice asked from behind the door. *"This shit gon be sweeter than I thought,"* Lil Rico thought to himself when he heard the female voice on the other side of the door.

Without getting any response, the female on the other side of the door opened the door. As soon as the door was completely opened, Reddot pointed his .357 in the Dominican beauty's face. *"Ay dios mio!"* she let out a scream.

"Shut the fucc up bitch! Who else in the apartment?" Reddot was the first to ask; the Dominican beauty was scared straight and was scared to make the slightest noise. *"Nobody, just me n my man,"* she said in her broke English.

"Lead to me to where that bitch ass nigga is at. If yuh make any funny move, I'm gon blow ya head off!" True Blue said loud enough for her to hear him. Without any hesitation the Dominican beauty escorted the three masked men in the direction of the back room.

Once in front of the room's door, True Blue and Lil Rico positioned themselves on each side of the room's door while Reddot kept the Dominican lady at gun point. *"Open the door mami."* Reddot whispered into the Dominican lady's ear, causing the hair on the back of her neck to stand up.

The Dominican lady didn't have any idea as to why this was taking place; all she hoped for was that she made it out it alive. After a few seconds, she finally pushed the room's door open.

As soon as the door was completely open, Lil Rico and True Blue rushed inside of the room catching the older Dominican man by surprise. *'BOOM! BOOM!'* True Blue let off two shots in the direction of the Dominican man who was only inches away from picking up the gun that was on the night stand next to the bed.

The two shots stopped him in his tracks as they hit the lamp on the night stand. *"The next one gon be on ya head papi,"* True Blue said meaning every word as they all entered the room. Lil Rico quickly made his way over to the night stand and picked up the loaded 9mm hand gun. *"Yuh won't be needin this,"* he sarcastically said to the Dominican man.

"Wat happen papi, mi no have no money here, watju want?" The Dominican man finally said in a thick Spanish accent. Reddot pushed the Dominican lady on to the floor and shot her twice in the back of her head. *'BOOM! BOOM!'*

Blood immediately started pouring onto the floor from the two quarter sized holes in the back of her head.

"Think we playin if yuh want papi, but as yuh can see we not," Reddot said with a smile on his face pointing the smoking .357 in his direction. *"Okay! Okay! No kill me, take everything is in the closet!"* The Dominican man said as tears rolled down his cheeks.

Without any second thought, Lil Rico walked over to the closet; and just like the Dominican man had said a few second ago. Everything was right there in the closet, on full display. *"Stupid mutherfuccer."* Lil Rico said out loud as he began to grab the bags of money and drugs out of the closet.

"See Papi, that wasn't that hard." True Blue said with a smile on his face. Nothing made him happier than a well done job. *"Si! Si! I no papi sorry, please no kill me, take everything me no care,"* the Dominican man cried out begging for his life.

"Nah papi I'm not gon kill yuh." True Blue responded as he and Lil Rico started making their way out of the room with the two duffle bags in hand. As soon as Lil Rico and True Blue were out of sight, Reddot walked over to where the Dominican man was sitting on the bed and shot him three times in his face. *BOOM! BOOM! BOOM!*

"Shit, he said he wasn't goin to kill, but I didn't!" Reddot said to the dead corpse before exiting the room and out of the apartment.

Chapter Twenty-Four

– Three Months Later –

It's been three months since True Blue and his crew went on the last robbery. After finding $70,000 in cash, three pounds of weed and six bricks of cocaine; they never looked back. Legend got in charge of all the weed.

True Blue and Lil Rico got in charge of the coke – turning the six bricks into ten. They decided to take four bricks and break it down into dimes, halves, quarters and twenties; the other six bricks they sold as weight – only to those they knew and dealt with.

The money on Hughes and Belmont Avenue was coming in nonstop. It got to the point wherein True Blue and Lil Rico had to open up shop in Prospect Avenue – True Blue's old block which was another gold mine.

Tired of paying for cabs and Ubers, True Blue and his crew decided to cop some wheels. True Blue jumped in a 2016 black on blackS550 Benz; with its peanut butter interior, he had it sitting on some custom 22 chrome rims.

Lil Rico copped a silver 2017 Chrysler 300 with an all-black leather seats and interior; he too had it sitting on some 22'; only difference was that his was custom black.

Boo hoped in the 2016 X5 BMW SUV, cocaine white with limo tints. He kept the rims that came with it. Last but not least, Legend opted for a black Cherokee jeep with a peanut butter interior and same peanut butter leather seats.

That wasn't all; not only were they all riding clean, True Blue had been hitting the recording studio heavy. The first track he recorded was called 'Come Again' and he featured Boo on that track. The song took off immediately.

'Come Again' had the strippers in the strip clubs going crazy. Promoters were calling nonstop trying to Book the two for shows; and the labels weren't too far behind trying to get them to sign the dotted lines.

Lefty had finally returned home from his parole violation. The trafficking charge was dismissed due to lack of evidence. True Blue no longer lived in Legend's house; he was now living with Aisha and her daughter in Courtland Avenue.

After finding out that Aisha was carrying his child, True Blue and Aisha decided that it would be best if they were all under one roof; and True Blue would not have wanted it any other way. The bond True Blue and Hailey shared was one of a kind and Aisha loved every second of it and so did True Blue.

A few weeks after hitting the Dominican spot, True Blue and his crew had gone on another 'lick' (robbery) and came up on an arsenal of weapon. You name it, they had it; from the smallest hand guns to the biggest riffles including bullet proof vests and ammunitions.

In order to avoid Legend's house being crammed full with all the weapons, they were looking forward to selling some of the new found merchandise. The money was coming in nonstop and niggas were starting to hate with capital 'H'. Capo had Alos join the team.

Capo's real name was Edwin Ruiz, he was 100 percent Dominican and stood 5 feet 8, 183lbs with a light skin complexion. Both of his arms and his stomach were covered with tattoos and his hair is sported in a low ceaser cut.

Capo also had a cut on the left side of his cheek from a previous fight. He was 30 years young and he was the lieutenant on Hughes Avenue drug operation. Reddot was promoted to do the pick-ups and drop-offs to Hughes, Belmont and Prospect Avenue. Reddot wasn't left out; he copped an all-black on black 2016 Dodge charger with the 3 percent tints on all of its windows.

It was November 6, 2016 and True Blue had his first show in Angels strip club in Queens, New York. True Blue glided the S550 down East Tremont and when he got to the corner on Author Avenue he made the right turn.

On getting to the 178th, True Blue made another right turn and the first person he spotted standing on the corner was Capo. A smile spread across his face seeing how hands-on Capo was with their business.

True Blue pulled the S550 into a parking space in front of Legend's building and hopped out. He made his way over to where Capo was standing in front of Big Homies' store as he lit the pre rolled blunt he had in his pockets.

"Ayo, Capo wats craccin cuhz?" True Blue said once he was only inches away from where Capo was standing. *"Oh shit, klok cuhz! Dime Ave?"* Capo shot back. *"Ain't shit, just came from wifey's crib,"* True Blue said taking a pull out of the blunt. *"Ayo yuh kno we got a show tonight right?"* he added passing Capo the blunt he was smoking on.

"Yeah I heard, but yuh kno I can't leave wit y'all niggas n leave the blocc unattended. I have to make sure shit runs how it's supposed to at all times. That's wat yuh pay me for cuhz." Capo stated; True Blue just looked at him for a few seconds admiring his work ethic.

"Yuh ain't never lie cuhz, but yuh kno that yuh can always pull up if yuh change ya mind loco." True Blue said

137

truthfully. After chopping it up with Capo, True Blue started making his way towards Legend's apartment.

- - -

– A Few Blocks Away –

"Ayo scrap! Yuh seen this shit? This nigga True Blue got a show tonight in Angels" Noni said to June while looking at the flier of True Blue's upcoming show on his FaceBook page. *"Oh word! Let me find out; them niggas gettin that show money now. Maybe we should slide by and show them niggas some love, if yuh kno wat I mean,"* June said with a smile on his face.

From time to time, Noni and June would go on for hours looking over True Blue and his crew's FaceBook pages in hopes of catching them locking; but they were never looking enough until today.

"Yuh kno wat? Maybe yuh have a point scrap! Look, hit Tommie n Lil Jay n tell them niggas I said we goin to the strip club tonight to make it rain on them hoes!" Noni finally said; after he finished rolling the blunt of loud, he lit it and took a few pulls of the joint.

Tommie and Lil Jay were twin brothers; they were both 19, but at only 19 years young, they both had a body count of six under their belt. Tommie and Lil Jay were also part of Noni's and June's organization.

139

- - -

– 11.00 PM Angel Strip Club –

True Blue and his crew pulled up to Angel's strip club two hours after it opened. The H-Blocc crews were four cars deep with True Blue's S550 leading the pack. Today, like any other show, Reddot rode shotgun in True Blue's S550. Reddot's job for the night was security.

As the four car parade made its way into the club's parking lot, all those that were waiting in line broke their neck dying to see the individuals who were inside the foreign cars. After pulling in back to back into their reserved parking space, the H-Blocc crew stepped out of their cars looking and feeling like money.

True Blue wore an all-black Balmain Denim with the matching black and silver sweat shirt. On his feet, he had a pair of all silver high top Mason Margiela sneakers. Around his neck he sported frozen water, as well as in his ears and wrist.

Lil Rico wore the opposite; his Gucci sweat suit alone cost $2,500. He wore a matching Gucci head band around his head; on his neck, ears and wrist, he wore the VVS Cuban link set.

Boo was dripped in Fendi. Legend was in Louis Vuitton. Reddot decided to keep it simple with his all black

140

Nike tech suit with matching Balenciaga sneakers on his feet. After a few minutes, the promoter finally stepped out and escorted them into the night club.

Due to the fact that the Harlem rapper Dave East was in attendance as well as Brooklyn's own Maino, the club was packed and lit. Once inside, True Blue and his crew were escorted into their VIP section.

True Blue and Dave East were in the same VIP section, while Maino was in the VIP section right next to theirs. *"Ayo cuhz, wats craccin? Congrats on ya new song loc, that's heat hit! Maybe we can put somethin together for the rmix!."* Dave East said loud enough for True Blue to hear him.

Dave East's latest single was playing out of the club's speakers. *"Yuh kno nigga like yuh n me! Good lookin cuhz n we can deff do that!"* True Blue shot back just as loud as Dave East was. They chopped it up for a little longer before they decided to order some bottles to get the party started.

"Yo Reddot, tell the waiter we need 20 bottles in this section, ten of D'usse n ten of Henny." True Blue turned around and whispered into Reddot's ears. On cue, Reddot went to go make the order.

Within minutes, the club was being lit up with the twenty sparkling bottles while Dave East and Juelz Santana's

'Times Tickin' ft. Bobby Shmurda came thumping out of the club's speakers. The strippers in attendance were nothing less than nine. Ass was everywhere as the strippers had their own contest as to who could shake the money maker better than the other.

"True Blue, Yuh about to be on deck! Yuh ready or yuh need some more time?" The promoter came and whispered into True Blue's ears. *"Nah loco I'm ready; when yuh are let me kno so I can turn this shit up!"* True Blue responded with excitement; he loved the feeling performing gave him.

"Aight bet, say no more! Be ready in ten," the promoter said before walking out of the VIP section. Fifteen minutes later, True Blue had taken the stage and was killing it. When 'Come Again' came pouring out of the club's speakers, the strippers started going crazy.

The song had turned the club upside down the same way it did it every time it came on. Ballers were throwing stacks of money like it didn't mean nothing and the strippers were loving every second of it; busting their best moves trying to outdo the other.

"Damn cuhz! Y'all niggas killed that shit!" Legend was the first to say when True Blue and Boo returned to the

142

VIP section. *"Good lookin cuhz, yuh kno how we do!"* True Blue shot back.

It was 3.00 am when True Blue and his crew had finally decided to leave the club. Their time there was well spent; they made a movie, their name was definitely going to be ringing a lot more than it already was after that epic night.

They made it to the parking and Reddot was on his job on all ten as he scanned the parking lot for any funny movement. He didn't see anything but for some reason he felt like something was off. Keeping his hand on his .357 he was ready for whatever.

The crew took a few steps before all hell broke loose and shots started flying in every direction breaking every car window that was near them. Instantly, they all ducked for cover behind the parked cars.

"Who the fucc is that?" True Blue was the first to say as he ducked behind the park car. *"I don't kno, but look; since I'm the only one strapped right now I'm gon try to keep these niggas off our ass. To give y'all enough time to get ya tan outta the car."* Reddot said, pulling his .357 out of his hoodie's pocket. On cue he stood up and returned fire.

BOOM!

BOOM!

BOOM!

True Blue, Lil Rico, Legend and Boo ran toward their cars to try to retrieve their weapon from their cars.

BOC!

BOC!

BOC!

BOOM!

BOOM!

The shooters were not letting up. They came to do a job and they didn't plan to abort the mission until the job was completed.

BOOM!

BOOM!

BOC!

BOC!

True Blue, Legend, Boo and Lil Rico rose up from behind their parked car guns blazing killing one of the closest shooter to them in the process. Seeing that they were no match to the five gun men; the shooters tried to run for cover behind a parked car.

BOOM!

BOOM!

Reddot let off another two shots hitting a second shooter in his back and on the back of his head before he was able to duck for cover behind a parked car; the shots killed him instantly. The shootout lasted for no longer than three minutes; but to them it felt like twenty minutes.

The parking lot of the club had turned into a total chaos as every party-goer was trying to avoid getting hit by a straight bullet. When the shooting had finally stopped, there were seven dead bodies. What had started out to be a nice night out ended up being a total nightmare to most of the party-goers.

The police now siren seemed to be getting closer by the minute. The two shooters that were left jumped back into their get-away car and raced off the scene. Almost immediately, True Blue and his crew followed suit.

Getting caught in a parking lot full of dead bodies was out of the equation. Out all of their cars, True Blue's S550 was the only one that pulled out of the club's parking lot not looking a slice of Swiss cheese.

- - -

"Fuck! Fuck! Fuck! How the fuck did them niggas get away witout one of them gettin fuckin touched" Noni yelled at June while he banged his fist on the steering wheel. *"I don't kno scrap! Them niggas must to have god on their side tonight."* June shot back as he held his bleeding knee cap.

"Aaggghhhh," June let out a moan as he tried to straighten his left leg. One of the bullets fired by True Blue and his crew had struck him on his left knee cap while he was trying to make his escape.

"I can't fuckin beleive this shit. Now Tommie n lil jay are gon over this shit!" Noni stated as he jumped back into the highway. 45 minutes later Noni pulled into the Lincoln hospital's parking lot on 149th street and 3rd Avenue in the Bronx.

As soon Noni dropped June off in the emergency room, he pulled off before the doctors were able to question him *"Y'all got away tonight, but I'm gon make sure y'all pay for everythin y'all did to me n mine!"* Noni thought to himself as he lit the blunt he had just finish rolling.

Chapter Twenty-Five

Santos 'Lefty' Gomez was 23 years young, stood 5 feet 9, 135lbs; with long silky hair which extends to the middle of his back. After coming home a few weeks ago, he wasted no time in getting back into what he knew best – pimping.

"I dont kno why y'all bitches in here sittin doin nothin, like there's no fuccin money to be made!" Lefty said stepping into the room. Lefty had a nice two bedroom apartment a few buildings down from where Legend's building was. *"Stop smokin up all my weed too."* Lefty added after seeing the blunt that Yari and Maiah were passing back and forth.

"Ohkay daddy n no, we not just sittin here. I already posted up not too long ago, now I'm just waiting on some hits". Mariah was the first to say. *"I'm talkin to someone as we speak. Everythin already set for when he gets out of work daddy."* Yari added.

Mariah Lopez was 21 years old. She was 5 feet 9, 165lbs with long jet black hair; she's thick in all the right places and has a cute face like the actress Jessica Alba but had the body of the rapper Fabulous' wife – Emely. Mariah was the true definition of BBW.

Yarisa 'Yari' Mendez was 24 years old; she stood 5 feet 7, 145 lbs with a light brown skin. She favors the actress

Sanaa Lathan to a 'T'. Her body had more curves then the letter 'S'. Yari was Lefty's bottom bitch because she brought in the most money out the pack. *"Oh, okay copy! That's wat I like to hear! dont forget to ..."*

"To stash the money once it's in our hands n text yuh the address." Mariah said cutting Lefty off, already knowing what Lefty was about to say; Lefty just looked at her with a smile on his face. *"Where is Sofie at?"* Lefty then asked as he lighted the blunt he had just finished rolling.

"Oh she out on a date, she wont be back till tomorrow mornin Daddy. She was Booked for the whole day today." Yari said, while adding some makeup to her beautiful face. Not too long after the words had left Yari's lips, a message came through in Lefty's phone. Looking at the phone, he smiled as he read the text from Sofia.

Sofia wasn't nothing like Yari nor Mariah, but she wasn't no slouch. Her beautiful face and body always had the tricks ready to trick. With no questions asked. It was just something about her that they couldn't seem to get enough off.

Lefty's phone started going off again, but this time it was with an incoming call. *"Yo wats craccin."* Lefty said into the receiver. *"Yo Lefty, where yuh at? I'm downstairs, I*

148

need four of them things." The voice on the other end of the phone said.

"Aight, bet I'm comin downstairs right now," Lefty responded. Lefty was not only in the pimping business; Thanks to True Blue and Lil Rico, he was now also in the drug business as well.

- - -

– Meanwhile ...–

Reddot woke up at 9:30am. It was Friday and like every other Friday, he had to make his rounds. It was 10.00am by the time Reddot had left his Castle Hill apartment. Jumping into his charger, he pulled out off the parking space and started to make his way over to Prospect Avenue.

Fifteen minutes later, Reddot was pulling up in front of Mike's building on Prospect and Dawson. Taking his phone out of the cup holder, he placed a call to Mike. *"Yo Mike, wats craccin cuhz? I'm down stairs."* Reddot said into the receiver when Mike answered.

"Aight copy bro." Mike shot back before ending the call. 'Times Tickin' by Dave East and Juelz Santana played out of the charger's speakers at a moderate level. A few minutes later, Mike finally walked out of his building with a brown paper bag in hand.

149

"Wats craccin Reddot!" Mike said when he entered the car. He handed Reddot the brown paper back. *"Thats all $30,000."* he then added. Without looking inside of the brown paper bag, Reddot placed it in the back seat.

"Copy loco, say no more. Look under that seat n grab that blue Channel bag. That's yuh. I'm gon get up out of here; I have to make another stop. Hit my line if anythin cuhz." Reddot said giving Mike some dap. As soon as Mike was out of the car, he pulled off.

It took Reddot twenty minutes to get from Prospect Avenue to Belmont Avenue. *"Yo fatboii I'm out front, bring that bread down. Hurry up too bcos I don't have time to waste!"* Reddot said into the receiver when Cavs answered; pissing him off.

Without saying a word Cavs ended the call. Reddot just looked at the dead phone and smiled. He loved getting under Cavs' skin every time he had the chance. *"Wats craccin fatboii?"* Reddot said when Cavs entered the car. In return, Cavs said nothing; he didn't have no rap for Reddot. In fact, he was still feeling salty about Reddot shooting him on his knee a few months ago.

"All ya bread is there; now give me my shit so I can shake the spot. I aint tryin to kick it with yuh for too long," was all that Cavs said when he finally spoke. Reddot looked

at him, he wanted to say something to him m but decided against it. He had another thing in my mind.

"Reach under ya seat n grabb that blacc Channel bag, thats yuh nigga." Reddot shot back. Cavs grabbed the bag as he was told and immediately swung the car's door open so he could step out; but as soon as only his right foot touched the pavement Reddot pulled off causing Cavs to fall on the floor and messing up his all white polo sweat suit.

Reddot stopped at the corner, looking in his rear view mirror; he couldn't help but to start laughing as he watched Cavs struggle to get up off the ground. After reaching over to close his car's door, he pulled off in the direction of H-Blocc to drop off the $70,000 he had just collected. 'It was $70,000 crody.' read the text that Reddot had sent True Blue.

Chapter Twenty-Six

Cavs sat inside of his trap smoking and thinking about how Reddot had disrespected him once again in front of his workers. While he thought about how he was going to deal with Reddot, C-Lite and Montana were stuck to the T.V. playing 2k16. *"I'm gon make sure he pays for the disrespect in due time."* Cavs said to himself as he exhaled the smoke out of his nostrils.

"Dime tribu, yuh just gon seat there thinkin about Reddot the whole day?" C-Lite turned around and asked, not understanding why Cavs was constantly letting Reddot get under his skin.

'Mask off' by Future played out of the small radio that sat on top of the kitchen counter. Cavs just looked at C-Lite without saying a word. From the look that Cavs had gave C-Lite, if looks could kill, C-Lite would have been dead. Cavs just continued to bob his head up and down as he listen to his favorite rapper – Future kill his latest track.

- - -

– A Few Blocks Away –

"Hey, so how are things with yuh n True Blue goin?" Eileen asked while she and Aisha were on their lunch break. *"Everythin's been good between us. He's really happy that*

he's havin his first born; he's always rubbin my stomach n talkin to the baby as if he could hear him." Aisha stated with smile on her face.

Things were going really well between Aisha and True Blue, and she wouldn't have wanted it any other way. *"Oh okay, cool! That's watssup! I'm happy for y'all. I can tell that he makes yuh happy."* Eileen replied. *"Yes he does, I just hope it stays like that, bcos I'm really feelin him n I can tell that he's feelin me just as much."* Aisha said.

They continued to enjoy their $7 special of white rice, beans and chicken stew from the El Valle restaurant on East Tremont. When the two sisters had finished their lunch, they paid for their food and left out of the restaurant and headed back to their places work.

Chapter Twenty-Seven

– Premo's Candle Lighting –

Today was Sunday, November 24th which is exactly a year that 'Premo' had passed. Premo was a Legend in his own right when it came to the Crips organization. Therefore everybody that was somebody came out to pay their respect to their fallen soldier.

H-Blocc was packed with seventy Crip members and it was only 2.00pm. Looking into Hughes Avenue from blocks away, the only thing that was visible was the all the blue that everyone in attendance wore. The streets were so crowded that the cars could barely make their way through Hughes.

Candles and Hennessey bottles were lined up against the blue wall where Premo's picture hung. The love was heavy in the air. Lil Rico and True Blue had made sure that even though their fallen soldier was gone, that he was never forgotten.

The 48th precinct was also on the scene; they were there to make sure nothing got out of hand.

- - -

– Meanwhile …–

"Ayo Trey ain't them niggas havin a candle lightin for Premo out there today?" Noni asked out of the blue while they were all in the trap smokin and sippin on some Hennessey. Ever since Lil Chris was killed, Noni felt like he's got nothing to live for. He lived everyday like if it was his last.

"Yeah they are, but yuh kno I cant let yuh go over there n disrespect my man Premo. Yeah i don't really fucc with them other niggas; but Premo was my main man loco." Trey quickly shot back, already knowing where Noni was going with the conversation.

"Plus goin over there right now would be a suicide mission. There's too many niggas out there right now." Trey then added. Noni just looked at Trey for a few seconds without saying anything.

"Yeah you right, I fucced with Premo too scrap. That's the only reason I really aint sliding through; I can careless about how many niggas are out there though." Noni finally said taking a sip out of the bottle of Hennessey he was sipping on. *"Out of respect for Premo, I'm gon fall bacc today"* he then added passing Trey the blunt they been smoking on.

- - -

– H-BLOCC –

It was already 5.00pm and the block was more crowded than what it was three hours ago. True Blue and his crew decided to end the day with going to Premo's gravesite. They had planned to smoke a few blunts with him as well as to drink a bottle of Hennessey with him.

It was 5:45pm when True Blue and his crew arrived at Premo's gravesite. True Blue, Boo, Legend, Lil Rico and Reddot stood around Premo's grave for a few seconds in silence; all lost in their own thoughts.

Legend didn't get the chance to meet Premo, but from all the good things he heard about him and the way his men treated him, he felt the need to show the same respect as they did.

"Damn loco, it's crazy how it's already been a year that the cuhz been gone," True Blue said, as he took the top off of the Hennessey bottle and poured some out for Premo. *"Yeah loco, tell me about it, shit crazy! I remember few days before the shit happened I was talkin to the cuhz n he said that he had everythin under control. I still can't believe that he got caught laccin like that."* Lil Rico stated taking a few pulls out of the blunt he had been smoking on.

They all had their own blunt to smoke including one for Premo. They were all feeling emotional, but were trying to hold it together because they knew that Premo wouldn't have wanted it any other way.

"That's why we have to live every day like is our last. Tomorrow aint promised to no one cuhz." Reddot added. Boo was taking it the worst out of the five. He was the last one who had been with Premo the day before he had passed. Premo was the one who thought him everything he knew about Cripin and now that his mentor was gone, he felt like a side of him was gone as well.

The crew ended staying in the cemetery until it was closing hour. After they were finished paying Premo their respect, they all jumped into their separate cars and made their way back to H-Blocc. Although Premo was gone, one thing for sure and two things for certain; neither Lil Rico nor True Blue would let his name, legacy and what he had done as a father and Crip be forgotten. Premo would forever live through them as long as they were alive.

Chapter Twenty-Eight

Today was a Sunday, and like every other Sunday, Legend was at the Lenny and Timmy's car wash on Westfarm Square and East Tremont. The weather was nice for a December morning. After confirming his jeep was clean and detailed, Legend paid the Mexican man for the good job he had done before jumping into his car and pulling out of the car wash.

Legend was dressed in an all money green Nike tech sweater and sweat pants. On his feet, he had on a pair of all black Jordan number 6s. As he cruised up East Tremont, Lil Baby's 'Yes Indeed' featuring Drake played out of the system.

"Fucc!" Legend said to himself as he got caught at the red light on the corner of East Tremont and Vyse Avenue. Legend sat in his jeep passionately waiting for the light to change from red back to green when he noticed a familiar face coming down East Tremont in the opposite direction.

As the person got closer Legend couldn't believe as to who he was staring at. Legend watched as the person turn into Vyse Avenue without a care in the world. *"Look at this nigga movin like shit fuccin sweet."* Legend said to himself.

When the light turned green, Legend made the right turn into Vyse Avenue in the same direction he had seen the person walking. He looked around for a few second before he spotted that same person making a turn in the corner into Daily Avenue.

"I wouldn't have wanted it any other way." Legend said out loud as he double parked his truck and hoped out. Looking around, he noticed that the block barely had any activities going on. *"Perfect,"* he thought.

After making sure that his 9mm was locked and loaded, Legend made his way up the block towards Daily Avenue; but, Legend wasn't prepared for what was waiting on him just as he turned into the corner.

BOOM!

BOOM!

BOOM!

As soon as the first three shots went off, Legend instantly ducked back behind the wall; while the three bullets that were fired in his direction missed his head by a half of an inch. *"Wat the fucc,"* Legend exclaimed, caught by surprise.

After getting himself together, Legend extended his right arm around the corner and let off four shots of his own. *BOC!*

BOC!

BOC!

BOC!

Hearing the shots coming from around the corner, the person Legend had been following ducked behind a parked car. *"Who the fucc is this nigga."* he said while letting off another two shots, trying to keep his enemy at bait.

BOOM!

BOOM!

It only took Legend a few seconds to notice that the weapon his target was carrying was nothing bigger then a .38 special and if that was the case, he knew that with the five shots he had already counted, that he should only have one left.

There was only one way to find out; Legend stepped around the corner, and like he expected his target let off another shot before his gun started clicking, indicating that there was no more live rounds left. Legend smiled to himself.

"I got ya bitch ass now!" Legend said loud enough for his target to hear him. Seeing that he was out of ammo, the target tried to make a run for his life; just what Legend had been waiting for the whole time. As soon as his target's body was fully exposed, Legend wasted no time on letting the 9mm do the talking.

BOC!

BOC!

BOC!

BOC!

BOC!

Legend missed the first three shots, but the other two shots found a home in the middle of his target's back causing him to stumble, head first, onto the pavement. Legend wasn't worried about running out of bullets, the 30 shots his Nina held was enough to get the job done.

By the time Legend reached his target, he was lying on his stomach, blood pouring out of the two gunshot wounds; while he coughed up blood out of his mouth. The two bullets that pierced his back had found a home in his spine paralyzing him on contact.

"Fucc yuh doin in this part of town nigga? Yuh kno yuh aint no good on this side cuhz!" Legend said while he was only inches away from his target and with the smoking gun in his hand aimed at his victim. *"It looks like yuh goin through a lot of pain, I'm gon do yuh a favor cuhz!"* He added as he emptied the rest of his shells into Blue Heff's face and body.

When the gun clicked back empty, Legend gave him the *'are you dead?'* kick before running off back in the direction of his jeep. After jumping in his jeep, Legend pulled off like nothing ever happened up East Tremont.

While he was making his way back to H-Blocc, the police and ambulance sirens could be heard racing toward the crime scene. Reaching over to his cup holder, he grabbed the blunt he had been smoking on prior to the incidence; lighting the blunt of loud, he took a deep puff out of it, inhaling and exhaling the smoke. *"Three more to go,"* he said to himself as he made the left turn into 178th street.

Chapter Twenty-Nine

The month of November was a crazy one for Lil Rico and his team. With the back and forth they were doing with the Fairmont Avenue niggas; the street of East Tremont had been on fire, which only made things worse. The money flow was slow due to all the police activities.

Legend was the one that wasn't affected by everything that was going on. On top of everything that was going on, Lil Rico and True Blue were in need of a new 'connect' badly. After Ed had gotten locked up, everything seemed to start to slow up for them.

The only way they were staying at flow with the drug game, was due to the licks Tsunami was lining up for them; but with all the bodies that were dropping, the police and the FBI were heavy on the streets of the Bronx trying to connect the dots.

Lil Rico wanted to get back to business as soon as possible, but he also understood that the only way that was going to happen was when the Fairmont niggas were dealt with once and for all.

On their last lick, Lil Rico and True Blue had come up on an arsenal of weapons on top of the $87,000 that they had also recovered from the robbery. So as to avoid Legend's apartment loaded with their new found merchandize. Lil

Rico and True Blue had plans on getting rid of some of the guns they found.

Today, being a Saturday, with the afternoon soon out; Lil Rico was parked in front of JC's barber shop on Belmont Avenue. A few days prior, Lil Rico had brought it to his attention that he had some guns on deck for sale and JC claimed that he knew someone that would be willing to buy it from him.

Twenty minutes later JC finally walked out of the barber's shop and made his way over to Lil Rico'c car. *"Damn cuhz, my fault for keepin yuh waitin. Shit busy as shit in there right now."* JC said when entered the car.

"Shit, yuh kno how it gets on the weekend cuhz, niggas gettin ready to party n shit." Lil Rico responded while pulling the car back into traffic. *"Dont worry, we aint goin far cuhz, just takin a spin while we chop it up,"* he added, making the left turn into East Tremont.

Lil Rico and JC chopped it up for no longer than ten minutes. Before Lil Rico and JC parted ways, JC had promised Lil Rico to link him up with his cousin Jay from Brooklyn.

- - -

– A Few Days Later ... –

"*Yo wats craccin? Who's this?*" Lil Rico said when he answered the phone. "*Ay is this Lil Rico?*" The voice on the other end of the receiver shot back. "*Who wants to kno nigga?*" Lil Rico retorted getting frustrated. "*This is Jay loco, I'm JC's cousin; he told me yuh needed to holla at me.*"

"*Oh! Yeah my bad loco! I ain't kno the number. I thought this was one of these opps playing games on my line. Watssup tho, talk to me nice.*" Lil Rico said. "*Aint shit, coolin on this side. My cousin had told me that yuh got something yuh want me to look at n I'm tryin to see if I can slide through there today if yuh aint busy?*" Jay shot back getting straight to the point.

"*Oh nah loco I ain't doin shit right now, niggas is playin in the crib today. If yuh want to pull up, I'll send yuh the addy.*" Lil Rico replied, taking the blunt that Legend was offering him. "*Copy loco, send me the addy,*" Jay responded before they ended the call.

When Lil Rico got off the phone with Jay, he sent him the address to Legend's building without wasting any time. "*Wats son talkin about.*" True Blue asked, as he paused the PS4 that was on. "*Son aint playin no games. He said that he tryin to pull up n cash out right now on niggas.*" Lil Rico replied excited at the fact that they had finally found a person to sell some of the guns to.

"Oh okay! Copy, say no more; let's put this shit together for the nigga hopefully he cop all three of these shit in one shot." True Blue said placing the controller on the bed while he got up from his seat. Walking over to the closet, True Blue grabbed the bag out of the closet that contained a shotgun, .22 revolver and a .380 with a silencer and enough ammunition to go to war with.

"Shit, I don't see why he wouldn't want this shit." Lil Rico said while holding the shotgun in his hands. *"This bitch bad!"* he added as he pointed the powerful weapon at an imaginary target.

"Yeah I kno we gon give him a deal that he can't refuse cuhz." True Blue said placing everything back inside of the green duffle bag. It took Jay 45 minutes to get from Brooklyn to the Bronx.

As soon as Jay got to Legend's apartment and saw the package that True Blue and Lil Rico had for him; he automatically fell in love with the powerful weapons. Especially with the .40 cal with the silencer attached to it.

Lil Rico and True Blue had let everything go for $4,500; and Jay couldn't have wanted it any other way. The deal was made and a new found friendship was also built. Jay, Lil Rico and True Blue would go on and continue to do business for months to come; the more business that they did, the more their friendship grew.

As soon as the deal was successfully sealed, Lil Rico and True Blue returned to Legend's apartment and continued to enjoy the rest of their night. Tsunami had called to inform True Blue that he had another lick lined for them. Hearing this had brought a smile to True Blue's face because that only meant more money was going to be added to their pockets.

Boo, Legend, Reddot, True Blue and Lil Rico were all inside of Legend's crib; smoking, drinking and having a good time while taking turns playing the PS4. By the time they ended up parting ways, they had smoked a half of ounce of grand daddy kush; and drank two bottles of Hennessey.

Chapter Thirty

Detective Gonsalez sat on his desk looking over some Police reports that were scattered all over his desk trying to find a lead on any of the unsolved murders. Not being able to find anything was taking a toll on him. Not only was the Feds snooping around, but his job was now also on the line.

While Detective Gonsalez was looking at one of the Police reports, his partner Detective Rosario stormed into their office slamming the door behind causing Detective Gonsalez to look up in his direction.

"Wat the hell is wrong yuh boy! Stormin in here like yuh aint got no damn sense!" Detective Gonsalez said looking at his partner like he was crazy. *"Yuh aint gon fuckin believe this! The captain wants us both in his office in five; n the word goin around is that he's takin us off the case."* Detective Rosario finally said while pasting back and forth in the small office.

"Where the hell did yuh get that kind of information from?" Detective Gonsalez retorted sitting up in his chair; hearing that he was about to be taken off his case had gotten his full attention.

"Thats the fuckin word goin around in the whole fuccin Precinct!" Detective Rosario shot back as he walked closer to the desk where Detective Gonsalez was sitting at.

"Calm down Ros, this must be a misunderstanding. Why don't we go see wat is it that he really wants?" Detective Gonsalez said as he got up from his seat.

Detective Gonsalez was trying to act as calm as possible on the outside, but on the inside his stomach was in knots. The two detectives got their self together before walking out of their office in the direction of their boss' office.

When they had reached the captain's office, they noticed that he was on a phone call. *"Well, I speak to yuh in a few, they just came into my office now. Don't worry I got it under control,"* the captain said before ending the call.

Focusing his attention on his two detectives, he said: *"Listen to what I'm about to tell the two of you. This wasn't my decision and if I had any say; I would have done things different."* The captain paused for a few second before he continued. *"I don't know any other way to say this. So I'm going to just say it. You two are no longer in charge of any of the murder cases. This ain't coming from me; this came from the higher ups. And like I told y'all before, I don't like people breathing on my neck. So to save my ass, I'm going to do what's best for us all. So I advise you two to stay away... very far away."*

"I can't fuckin believe this shit! How yuh just gon take us off the cases we been working our asses off for!" Detective Rosario was the first to say slamming his fist on the captain's desk; not caring one bit about the disrespect.

"Yeah how the fuck yuh let that happen! This is fuckin unbelievable! After all we have done for yuh n this fuckin Precinct!" Detective Gonsalez finally said not being able to hold back his emotion any longer.

"How dare yuh two come into my fuckin office like y'all don't have no fuckin sense! I been told yuh two son of a bitches to get y'all fuckin shit together. If y'all would have listened to me, then yuh guys wouldn't be in this situation. It's been fuckin four months since the first murder happened and we still don't fuckin have a lead on any one of them! So don't come into my fuckin office talkin about yuh did this n that! Like I said this is out of my hands n the DEA and FBI had taken over every murder case we have!" The captain retorted with the same hostility the two detectives had exhibited.

Without saying another word, the two detectives stormed out of the captain's office lost in their own thoughts, feeling betray and played. Passing their office, they walked right out of the Precinct heated with none of them saying a word to one another.

170

"If these niggas think that they can just get rid of us like we some trash, they got another thing comin! Because I aint goin for none of that shit! Believe that!" Detective Gonsalez finally said, taking two deep pulls out of his Newport one hundred.

"Watever yuh have in mind partner, just kno that I'm with yuh 100%. How the fuck we lookin lettin some outsider come in here tellin us wat we can do or cannot do. They got us fucked up!" Detective Rosario stated, letting his partner know that he was backing him on whatever play he had in mind.

"Don't worry I'll think of somethin, n when I do, we gon take things into our own hands." Detective Gonsalez stated. Without saying another word Detective Gonsalez started walking in the direction of their squad car, Detective Rosario wasn't too far behind.

Once they were both inside of the car, Detective Gonsalez put the car in gear and raced out of the 48th Precinct's parking lot, like a bat out of hell; mad was a understatement, they were ready to kill anybody that got in their way if need be.

171

Chapter Thirty-One

– December 27^{th,} 2016 –

"Ooooooohhhh! Papppiiii! Ya dick feeeeellls sooo goooodd!" Aisha moaned while True Blue penetrated her in the doggy style position. True Blue had Aisha with her face buried in the pillows while he long stroked her from the back; given her all of his 7 and half inches, at the same time he stuck his thumb in and out of her butt taking her to another level.

"Oh my gawd!" Aisha added, loving the way True Blue was fucking her. The more Aisha cried out in ecstasy, the more True Blue dug in her gut. True Blue and Aisha had been going at for the past forty-five minutes; fucking each other in positions that were unheard of. They were both covered in sweat.

"Damn baby this pussy wet!" True Blue said as he watched his dick drench with Aisha's wetness every time it when in and came back out. *"Oh babbby, I'm-i-iii-im-bout to cummmm!!!"* Aisha let out another moan releasing her love juice all over True Blue's dick and stomach.

'Splack! Splack! Splack!' was all that was heard in their bedroom as True Blue continued to pump in and out bringing himself closer to his own orgasm. *"Aghhhh! Damn*

m-a-maaa!" True Blue moaned releasing himself deep inside of Aisha's pussy.

After giving Aisha two final strokes, True Blue pulled out of her love tunnel. Wasting no time, Aisha got on all four and guided his still erect penis into her mouth. Aisha started sucking on it, licking it, and jerkin it back and forth making sure True Blue released every drop of semen out of his dick.

"Pop!" was the sound that Aisha's mouth made when she finally released True Blue's dick. *"Happy birthday daddy!"* Aisha finally said whipping her mouth with the back of her hands. Being sure that True Blue was satisfied, she rolled out of the bed; making her way out of the room, she walked into the bathroom to get ready for work.

Since Aisha had to go to work, True Blue decided to spend his day with his crew until Aisha got out of work. They had planned to go to the City Island for Dinner when Aisha returned from the day's work.

- - -

– 3 Hours Later … –

True Blue pulled up to the front of 620. After finding a parking spot, he parked and exited his car looking a like a bag of money dressed in his all red and green Gucci outfit;

on his feet, he had a pair of high top red and green Gucci sneakers.

After locking his car's doors, True Blue walked into Legend's building. *"Ayo C! West craccin locos! Fucc y'all niggas in here doin?"* True Blue said as he entered Legend's room. *"Ohh! Look who's finally here! Happy fuccin cday cuhz!"* Boo was the first to say getting up from the small couch in the corner of Legend's room, embracing True Blue in a manly hug.

"Thank yuh cuhz! Real shit, thank yuh!" True Blue responded. *"Yeah, happy cday nigga!"* Lil Rico finally said. *"We fuccin turnin the fucc up!"* he added. *"Yeah! Happy cday crodie!"* Legend said, handing True Blue a stack of hundred dollar bills. *"I kno that aint much to a balla like yuh, but I hope it come in handy. That's 5 bands right there cuhz,"* he then added.

"Come on cuhz, it's not even about the money it's the thought that counts cuhz." True Blue said in response while giving Legend some dap. *"Ohh shit! The birthday boy in the fuccin buildin!"* True Blue heard a voice from behind say, catching him by surprise. Turning around he came face to face with Trey.

"Oh shit cuhz! I aint even kno yuh was in the spot!" True Blue shot back giving Trey some dap. *"Yeah I been*

174

here for a lil while, I had received a call so I stepped into the bacc room to take it," Trey replied, *"but I'm about to shake the spot. Happy cday cuhz, hope y'all niggas have a good one today!"* Trey added.

"Good lookin cuhz, n we sure will nigga; believe that!" True Blue responded *"Ayo, let's go cop a bottle of that Henny to get the party started!"* Boo said as soon as Trey left the apartment; ready to get his drink on. *"I kno we goin to City Island tonight, but that's four hours from now,"* he added; looking at the time on his watch. It read 3:45pm. *"Yeah, we can deff do that."* Legend added rubbing his hands together also ready to get his drink on.

- - -

– Meanwhile ... –

"Man, this nigga said that them niggas would be outside any minute n it's been 20 minutes n none of them niggas stepped outside yet. Watssup with ya men?" June asked Noni. Noni and June had been parked on the corner of Hughes and 178th street for the past hour waiting on True Blue or any of his men to show their face.

"Man! Calm ya ass down nigga. If he said that them niggas is there; then them niggas is there. We just have to fall back n let things play the fuck out." Noni retorted

175

annoyed by all the whining that June was doing since they got there.

"Well, them niggas need to hurry the fuck up scrap. I aint tryin to seat on this hot ass block with two pistols in the car like shit sweet." June shot back not caring about anything that Noni had said. Just as the words left his mouth, the door to 620 opened.

- - -

True Blue's phone rang and he answered on the second ring. *"Watssup Kay, talk to me nice."* True Blue said already knowing who it was that was calling. *"Hey Trueeeeeeeeee! Happy cday!"* Kay responded. *"Bobby is on the line, hold on let me connect y'all,"* she added.

Kay was the GS9 Records PR and also a good friend of Bobby. It was through her that True Blue and Bobby kept in contact. *"Ahh! Ahhh! Ahhhhh! West craccin cuhz! Happy fuccin cday my loc!"* Bobby Shmurda said into the receiver. *"Glllllllllllltt! Yuh kno niggas like us cuhz! Thank yuh my guy,"* True Blue responded with excitement. *"Talk to me nice cuzzo,"* he added.

"Nah, I'm just callin to let yuh kno that yuh killed that tracc I sent yuh. I also heard that yuh had a show the other day n that the shit was litty! I'm happy for yuh cuhz.

176

I'm tellin yuh, if yuh keep doin wat yuh doin; I'm gon make sure that yuh get ya'self a deal: but I need yuh to stay out the way while I work this deal with Epic Records." Bobby Shmurda said, getting straight to the point.

"That's love cuhz, I really appreciate yuh doin this for me cuhz; real nigga shit. Yuh gon see I'm gone take this shit to the moon; n yeah that shit wasn't nothing cuhz. Every tracc yuh sent me, I'm gon body it!" True Blue shot back. True Blue and Bobby continued to chop it up for the remainder of the call.

After Bobby had gotten off the phone; True Blue thanked Kay before ending the call. Not too long after, True Blue and his crew decided to head out to the liquor store that was located on East Tremont.

Boo was the first one to step out of the building. Not paying attention to his surrounding as he spoke to True Blue. Legend was the last one out of the building since he had to make sure he locked the apartment door behind him. *"Yo cuhz ..."* Boo started to say, but was cut off by the gun fire which came out of nowhere.

BOOM!

BOOM!

BOOM!

BOC! BOC! BOC! BOC!

BOOM!

BOOM!

Bullets were flying everywhere, tearing up everything in its way. Not knowing where the shots were coming from. True Blue, Legend, Boo and Lil Rico ducked as low as they could and ran back inside of the building. *"Agghhh!!!"* True Blue moaned in pain as he felt a slug penetrate his Gucci sneakers finding a home right above his left pinky toe.

Luckily for them, the door was still open due to the fact that a soda cap was holding it open. They always kept a soda cap on the door for easy access back into the building in case anything was to ever happen.

The two shooters didn't stop there though; they continued to shoot their guns until it kicked back empty. Neither of True Blue, Legend, Lil Rico nor Boo was able to act fast enough to return any fire being that they were caught off guard.

Getting back inside of Legend apartment, True Blue instantly took off his sneakers and just like he expected he had a hole the size of a dime right above his left pinky toe; his socks and sneakers were drench in his blood. Lil Rico sat to the far end of the room, still not believing that they really came close to losing their lives because they got caught slipping.

Legend on the other hand couldn't understand how was it that the shooters knew exactly where they were at or better yet, that they was coming outside at the time that they did. He didn't have all the facts, but if he had to take a wild guess. Trey would be the only one to blame.

Although the shot to his foot wasn't life threatening; True Blue was in serious pain as his foot kept getting swollen by the minute. He couldn't believe that on his 'born day', he came so close to dying.

Through the pain and all, neither True Blue nor his team let that stop their plans for the night as promised; they ended up still going to City Island. The pain in True Blue's foot only got worse, but so as not to spoil the night he, acted and moved like everything was fine, when it really wasn't.

Chapter Thirty-Two

– Days Later –

Neither True Blue nor his crew looked back after their last stick up. Although Tsunami didn't want anything in return, True Blue and Lil Rico still broke him off with $15,000. They both felt like that was the least that they could have done, since he was the one that set everything up for them.

The money was coming in hand over fist once again. The only problem the crew had was that they didn't know how to save for the rainy days; as fast as the money came was as fast as it went.

As promised, JC's cousin, Jay has been coming nonstop; taking whatever gun he wanted to get out of their hands. That only added to the stack of money that they were already getting off the block. On his last trip, Jay had bought a SKS with a hundred round drum on it and an AK47 with a sixty two shot banana clip.

Life was good for the brothers and their crew. They wouldn't have wanted it any other way. The way Jay was buying guns; you would have thought that he was at war with a small army. Neither True Blue nor Lil Rico cared about who he was beefing with; as long as his money was correct.

Every time he came to see them, they would make sure that he left with whatever he wanted.

- - -

– Meanwhile … –

"Ayo, I aint gon lie; I'm fuckin tired of sittin in this fuckin crib my guy! Why the fuck we have to lay low like we some kind of bitches or something," June said while taking a few pulls out of the blunt he and Noni had been smoking on.

Ever since they pulled the move on True Blue and his crew; they had been laying low. Not because they were scared, but because they were smarter than that; they both knew that True Blue and his crew would be out all day and night trying to retaliate for the attempt on their life.

"Man, we can't just be out there standing like shit sweet scrap. The boys are out there heavy n on top of all that; them niggas probably out there lurking. I mean, I ain't scared of them niggas, but we have to play this shit smart if we plan to be the last ones standin when the smoke clears," Noni responded making June see the logic in why they were laying low.

"Yeah yuh, have a point there scrap, I ain't even gon front." June shot back, seeing the bigger picture.

- - -

Lil Rico navigated his Chrysler 300 through the cross Bronx express way. He was on his way to the Throughneck section of the Bronx to see his boo thang 'Frahelis'. With everything that was going on, it's been a little while since they had spent any time together. Not only had Lil Rico missed her, but it was also time for him to release some stress.

With all the back and forth that was going on, Lil Rico haven't been able to burst a nut in over a month. With all the chaos going on, pussy was the last thing on his mind; staying above the ground was his main priority.

Chapter Thirty-Three

Boo and Star have been in the Co-Up city mall for the past three hours shopping for a baby's crib. Star was four months pregnant and she was beginning to show. Boo was already tired of all the walking around they were doing. On top of that, they still haven't found the crib they were looking for.

"Babe, if we haven't found it yet, it's because they don't have it here. We already got the clothes out of the way. We can come bacc for the crib another day or tomorrow. I'll take yuh to the cross county mall." Boo said, hoping that Star didn't buck his request because he was tired and wasn't really trying to argue.

Ever since Star found that she was pregnant, everything turned into arguments. Star stopped in her track and turned around to face Boo. *"Here she goes,"* Boo thought to himself. *"Babe, I kno yuh must be tired n I aint even gon lie, my feet hurts from all the walkin we been doin. I think we should call it a day as well, but yuh still gon have to take me to the cross county mall tomorrow because I need to get my baby his crib."* Star finally said.

"Okay baby, that shit aint about nothing. Yuh kno I'm gon take yuh early in the mornin to get it out the way," Boo responded. After paying for the clothes that they had purchased Boo and Star exited the mall.

When they got to the mall' sparking lot, Boo and Star walked in the direction of Boo's X5. Boo hit the key chain and the truck's trunk popped open. Placing the bags in the trunk, Boo hit the button on the key chain once more making the door shut close.

Walking around to the driver's seat, the car that had passed by had caught his attention; something about the car and the voice of the driver sounded too familiar. By the time Boo turned back around, the car had already pulled into an open parking space.

After entering his car, Boo decided to stick around before pulling off to see who the driver of the car was. After a few minutes, Boo was finally able to see who the driver of the car was. Boo couldn't believe it; he thought that his eyes were playing tricks on him, but they weren't it was him...

- - -

"Babe, that bitch is lyin. How the fuck yuh gon take that bitch's words over mine?" June asked pulling into the vacant parking space. *"Yuh act like this is the first time I caught ya ass cheatin nigga! That's why I don't know why I'm even still with ya ass now. Yuh think because yuh take me on shoppin sprees, that I'm suppose to forget the shit yuh be out here doin when yuh aint with me."* Erica, June's girl said.

184

"Babe, I'm sorry for all the things I put yuh through; but I love yuh ma n I want us to be together. I'm gon change, just please bear with me." June pleaded his case. Without saying another word, Erica exited June's car; mad or not she wasn't going to turn down a free shopping spree. June followed her lead; getting out of the car, they both walked into the Channel store.

- - -

"Babe, who are we waitin for? I'm tired n I'm ready to go." Star asked, not understanding why they were still in the mall's parking lot. *"Yeah, I kno babe, but I have to take care of somethin real quicc n then we can go I promise baby."* Boo quickly said. He was just as tired as Star was, but he couldn't let the opportunity pass; because he doesn't know when it would come back around.

An hour later, June and Erica walked out of the mall holding hands. The argument they were having prior to entering the store was no longer the topic. After June had spent $10,000 on her, all she wanted to do was get home to fuck her man dry.

Boo kept his eyes on the couple until they reached their car. When they had both entered June's car, Boo made his move. *"Look babe, I'm gon need yuh to jump in the driver seat while I take care of somethin. As soon as I hop bacc in the car get us the fucc out of here okay."* Star shook her head up and down without saying a word.

Star already knew what Boo was getting at. In a couple of situations, Star had been Boo's driver. Boo hoped out of the car and slowly jogged in the direction of June's car. As he approached the car, to his surprise, he noticed that Erica's head was buried in June's lap.

Seeing a reflection through his peripheral, June turned in its direction. When he made eye contact with Boo, his heart skipped a beat. Wasting no time, Boo raised his gun into the car through the open window and fired.

BOOM!

BOOM!

BOOM!

BOOM!

BOOM!

BOOM!

BOOM!

BOOM!

The sound of the gun shots caused the parking lot full of shoppers to go into total chaos as the shoppers tried to run and hide to avoid getting hit by a straight bullet. The eight shots that Boo fired had found home into both June's and Erica's body, killing them instantly.

BOOM!

BOOM!

Boo let off another two shots before making his escape. As he hopped in his car, just like he had instructed, Star pulled out of the parking space and blended in with the rest of the cars that were running off the scene.

- - -

"Hi, my name is Lisa Even from Bronx 12 news and I'm here in front of the Co-Up city mall where witnesses said that out of nowhere, shots started going off. What started out to be a nice December day, turned out to be shoppers' worst nightmare. When the Police arrived on the scene, they discovered a male and a female both shot dead inside of their vehicle. Police still don't know what was the motive as of yet nor do they have any suspects in custody. If..."

After hearing all he needed to hear, Boo shut the TV off. Getting up from his liven room couch, he made his way in the direction of his room. *"Shit, one down; one more to go."* Boo thought to himself as he entered his room.

Chapter Thirty-Four

"Babe, do yuh kno where I put the paper n fronto at?" Reddot asked Diamond. Reddot and Diamond had just finished having round of some hot steamy sex. Now they were trying to get their mind right of some grand daddy kush.

"No babe, I last saw it on the dresser but it wasn't much. I think we done smoke it already babe," Diamond replied, still trying to catch her breath. *"Damn!"* Reddot said, getting up from the bed to look for the paper and fronto on the dresser. After two minutes of looking for it he came to the conclusion that they were out of paper and fronto.

"I think we ran through that shit too ma, I'm about to go down n get us some so that we can smoke." Reddot stated. Walking over to the side of the bed, he picked up his jeans and slid them on. After putting on his sneakers, he grabbed his hoodie and keys and walked out of the room. Patting his waist, he noticed that he didn't have his .357, he thought about going back for it, but then decided not to since he wasn't going too far.

Reddot and Diamond lived in the Castle Hill section of the Bronx; an area known to be the home of the Sex, Money and Murder Bloods. They have been living in Castle Hill for the past two years and even though Reddot was a

Crip, he never had any issues since he had been living there. Walking out of his apartment, Reddot walked over to the elevator and stepped in.

- - -

"I ain't gon lie, shit break city out here today scrap!" Timmie Blazer said. *"Yuh ain't never lie blood, but I don't care how cold it is, I'm still gon be out here get to that bag! That cold shit don't face me blood,"* Jo-Jo shot back rubbing his hands together trying to keep them warm.

"Shit, fucc all that, I'm about to take my ass inside the store; a nigga's feet cold as shit!" Loonie, the younger out the crew said. Timmie Blazer was the big homie of every sex money member in the Castle Hill section of the Bronx.

At only 26 years old, Timmie Blazer had already racked up a mountain of bodies under his belt. He demanded respect wherever he went and those who thought otherwise always came up missing. Jo-Jo and Loonie were his little homies.

"Ayo, who the fuck is that comin up the block with all that fly shit on?" Jo-Jo asked Timmie who turned around in the direction that Jo-Jo was looking in. *"I don't kno scrap, but we about to find out right now. It looks like he's comin in this direction,"* Timmie replied.

189

- - -

"Damn! I should have brought my piece with me." Reddot thought to himself just as he spotted the four bloods standing in front of the Deli Grocery Store. Without saying a word, Reddot walked by them and went into the store. As soon as he entered the store, Reddot walked over to the counter to place his order.

"Yoock, let me get a pacc of some dark fronto with some Bob Marley rollin papers; and let me get a pacc of M&Ms too." Reddot said to the Ock that was behind the counter. After he paid for his items, Reddot left out of the store. Reddot was one heavy Crip time; he never left his apartment without his blue rag. Today wasn't any different, his blue rag hung freely out of hit left back-pocket.

"Ayo, yuh kno yuh in the wrong place, wearin that flew rag homie." Reddot heard someone say from behind him. Not being one to take any disrespect lightly, Reddot stopped in his tracks and turned around. *"Yuh got me fucced up cuhz! I go wherever I please with my blue rag cuhz. I dont care about y'all niggas, but this is Crip over here!"* Reddot shot back, stocking his set with his fingers for emphasis.

"Nah nigga, the only one that got shit fucced up is yuh scrap! This is Blood over here and like I said nigga, yuh in the wrong place homie." Timmie Blazer said, as Jo-Jo and

190

Loonie stood on the right and left side of him; ready to prove something to their big homie. Seeing what was about to take place Reddot mentally prepared himself for the worst.

"Nah nigga! Yuh must be hard at listenin!" Reddot retorted. Tired of the back and forth, Timmie took off on Reddot catching him with a left hook right on his chin. The blow didn't face Reddot as much as Timmie thought it would.

Reddot tried to take a swing at Timmie but was stop in his tracks as another punch caught him on the right side of his head and then other one on the left side of his eyes. It didn't take long for Reddot to know what was going down. He was getting jumped. Reddot was a great fighter but he wasn't no match for his three assailants.

When it was all said and done, Reddot left out of the fight with a slit above his left eyebrow, a busted lip and a black eye; something that he wasn't too happy about and planned on getting Timmie and his goons back for the disrespect.

"Oh my gawd! Baby, wat happen to ya face!" Diamond asked with much concern when Reddot stepped into their room with blood all over his hoodie. Without saying a word, Reddot walked over to his dresser, opened the drawer and grabbed hisv.357 out of it.

191

When he had confirmed that it was fully loaded he made his way right out of the room. *"I'm fine babe, don't worry ya'self too much; this shit aint about nothing,"* was all that Reddot said before walking out of the apartment.

- - -

"Where the fuck that hardback nigga thought he was? He got niggas over here fucced up frfr!" Jo-Jo said excited that he had finally put in some work with his big homie. *"Yo yuh seen how I caught that nigga with that left hook? I'm sure that shit rocked that niggas brain!"* Loonie said, also excited about putting in work with the hood Legend – Timmie Blazer.

"Yeah, I bet that nigga aint gon be comin bac through here with all that dumb shit." Timmie finally said. *"Oh, so y'all niggas really thought, y'all was just gon whoop me n sit here n laugh about it."* Reddot said catching Timmie, Jo-Jo and Loonie by surprise.

"See the different between me n y'all niggas is that I always finish the job. Y'all did y'all thing but forgot one thing; to finish the job!" With that said, Reddot fired his .357.

BOOM!

BOOM!

The shots hit Timmie in his face and in his upper chest; killing him instantly. Jo-Jo tried to run in the opposite direction; Reddot quickly aimed the smoking .357 in his direction and fired.

BOOM!

The shot hit Jo-Jo in the back of his head causing him to do a front flip. Loonie almost got away, but he wasn't able to out run the bullets that came out of Reddot's .357. Seeing Loonie hit the floor, Reddot jogged up on him. *"Please don't kill me, "* Loonie begged for his life.

"Oh now it's please don't kill yuh huh? Fucc out of here nigga. Yuh aint so tough now I see." Reddot said with a smile on his face. Tired of all the begging, Reddot let the final bullet tear through Loonie's nose, leaving a hole the size of a quarter in the middle of his face.

Throwing his hoodie over his head, Reddot jogged in the direction where his car was parked at. *"These niggas got me fucced up."* Reddot said to himself when he had entered his car. As he was pulling out of his parking space, the Police siren could be heard getting closer and closer by the minute.

193

Chapter Thirty-Five

It was 9:45pm, True Blue and Lil Rico sat parked in the Secor Projects waiting on Tsuami to arrive. Tsunami had come through once again. A few minutes had gone by before Tsunami and his female friend finally walked out of the back door of his building.

Spotting True Blue's car, they both made their way over to the car. True Blue no longer had the S550 due to the shooting that took place in Angels Gentlemen club's parking lot; he now drives a 2017 BMW 750li.

"Klok my brother!" Tsunami said as he approached the driver's side window. *"Na aqui tu sabe chillin. Ready to get this shit over with so I can head bacc home to my lady,"* True Blue said back. *"Get in the car loco,"* he added. Tsunami did as he was told.

"Yo, this is the shorty I was talkin to yuh about," Tsunami started to say. *"This is the only way we can get him to open the door. They tried to rob him before so after a certain time he doesn't open the door for anyone. So, we need her,"* he added.

"That shit aint about nothin; but shorty better be good money loco bcos I aint tryin to get Booked over this shit cuhz." Lil Rico said. *"Nah loco, she good; trust me, I kno her."* Tsunami quickly said defending his friend.

194

"Oh aight copy, say no more then" Lil Rico responded. *"Okay, so listen; this is how this shit gotta go...."* Tsunami went on to explain in detail everything about the person they were robbing and about the $56,000 in cash and the 6 bricks that were also supposed to be in the spot.

The person they were robbing was a Dominican dude that went by the name Jose. He was the projects' 'grocery store.' Anything and everything you wanted, he had it. The local store was a mile away from the Projects; that fact alone made his business that much successful. Nobody wanted to take the mile ride or walk when they had a store right in the Projects.

"Copy say no more loco, consider that shit done. We gon call yuhas soon as the job gets done loco." True Blue assured Tsunami. *"Tato loco, say no more."* Tsunami shot back. If he doesn't know anything, one thing he knows was that he got the right niggas to get the job done.

- - -

"Who is it?" A male voce yelled from behind the closed door. *"Its me Jeny, I'm tryin to cop myself a 8th."* Jeny shot back. True Blue and Lil Rico stood on both side of the door waiting for the door to be open so they can make their move.

195

"Jeny yuh a lil late! Yuh kno I dont fuck around at this time," the man behind the door said. *"Yeah I kno, but I'm just now gettin out of work; I had to work a double shift tonight."* Jeny quickly said. *"Oh damn, I'm gon do this one time for yuh Jeny, but never again, okay?"* The man said from behind the door as he unlocked it.

As soon as the door was completely opened, True Blue and Lil Rico made their move. *"Don't fuccin move papi!"* True Blue said as he pointed his .38 special directly in the man's face. The man was caught by surprise. He was kicking himself in the ass for not standing on is word.

"Yeah papi don't fuccin move nigga!" Lil Rico added as he took a step closer. Even though Jose was being held at gun point, deep down in his mind, he wasn't willing to go out without a fight: so he did the unthinkable.

Jose grabbed True Blue's gun by the nose and they both started tussling for the gun. Jose held the nose of the gun with his dear life, trying to get it loose from True Blue's hand; but True Blue wasn't going for it.

True Blue knew that the man was way stronger than him and that if he kept tussling with him, the man would eventually get the gun out his hands. Lil Rico was on Jose's line raining blows after blow on his face and head, but Jose still wasn't ready to let go of the gun.

Tired of the back and forth, True Blue squeezed the trigger. *"BOOM! BOOM!"* The first shot caught Jose dead in the palms of his hand as the second shot caught him in his left leg. *"Aagggghhhhh!"* Jose let out a moan in pain; he immediately let the gun go.

True Blue raised the gun and fired. *"BOOM! BOOM! BOOM!"* The three shots found a home in Jose's upper chest and neck; causing him to fall backwards onto the floor. *"I told ya bitch ass to let the gun go!"* True Blue said in rage.

"Dadddddddyyyyy!!!" True Blue and Lil Rico heard a little girl yell from the apartment's hallway. That was their cue to get the hell out of there. Back in the car True Blue and Lil Rico couldn't believe the turn of event as they drove out of the parking lot.

True Blue and Lil Rico were beyond mad, the fact that they were leaving without what they had come for was something that they could have charged to the game; but the fact that they had just caught a dumb body was weighing heavy on their mind because they didn't know if Tsunami's friend was going to be able to hold water if worst came to worst.

197

Chapter Thirty-Six

– FBI HEAD QUARTERS, NY –

"Good morning ladies and gentlemen! I brought you all here today to give you all an update on the Hughes Avenue DTO. These seven individuals are not only infecting our streets with the poison that they are selling but they are also making our society more dangerous by also putting illegal guns into our community."

The chief of FBI paused before he continued, trying to make sure that all the agents in attendance were following him. *"Thanks to agents like Thomas 'Jay' Rodriguez and agent Damien 'Cuhz' Weaver; we have been able to keep a close tab on our main targets,"* he continued.

The FBI boss further said *"Thanks to our CI-1; we were able to find out that Alex 'Lil Rico' Valdez and Andy 'True Blue' Acosta are the leaders of the Hughes Avenue DTO. During the course of six months, our agents were able to purchase several firearms, including a SKS with a hundred round magazines, AK47s, shotguns, and multiple handguns with a silencer as well."*

Speaking further, the FBI chief warned that *"these seven individuals are not to be taken lightly; as you see, they are out here in these Bronx streets with military weapons.*

Acosta and Valdez are also members of the "Rolling 30s" neighborhood set of the nationwide Crip street gang. They not only members, they are also two high ranks in the set."

"When dealing with these individuals we are going to take every precaution needed and when we finally move in on them, remember, safety would always be our main priority." The FBI chief said in conclusion; adding that, *"I want you all to take your time studying these individuals; we are aiming to close this investigation by August 9th, 2017. With that being said, this meeting is adjourned. The next time we meet, we would be getting ready to move in."*

After the chief of the FBI finished saying his speech, he stepped down from the podium. On his way out of the conference room, he shook a few hands. Once the chief was of sight, all the agents in attendance also exited the conference room.

Chapter Thirty-Seven

– April 20th, 2017 –

Today wasn't as cold as it was a few days ago. Legend stood in front of big homies store wearing a pair of all white and blue Nike sweat short's with a pair of fresh out the box Airforce 1s and an all-blue Nike T-shirt to match. Today was April 20th, and Legend's phone has been going off since the moment he woke up.

Every pod head wanted to get their hands on that new grand daddy kush that Legend had. Although the money was coming in hands over fist, Legend had a bad feeling in the pit of his stomach due to that fact alone he decided to make sure that he doesn't leave out of his apartment with his new toy, his 30 shots F&N.

Legend looked up and down Hughes Avenue, looking out for any D-boy (Detective.) Getting caught for a sale on 4-20 was not in his plans. *"Damn, why the fucc this nigga comin over here for?"* Legend thought to himself has he spotted Trey turn the corner on East Tremont into Hughes Avenue.

"Wats craccin cuhz, I see yuh aint playin no game, yuh out here bright n early I see." Trey said once he was only a few feet away from Legend. *"Yeah, yuh kno me cuhz,*

the money dont sleep, so Legend cant rest." Legend replied, using Lil Wayne's line from the song 'John'.

Legend ain't like Trey, not one bit because he always felt like he was up to no good; but the fact that he was True Blue and Lil Rico's homeboy was the only reason as to why Legend tolerated him. *"Yeah, I feel yuh on that; where the locs at?"* Trey said back. *"Them niggas had something to do, it's just me on the blocc today."* Legend said, as he served one of his customers.

"Oh okay copy. Ayo, let me have two 8ths of that grand daddy kush yuh just got." Trey stated. *"I got these two lil mamis waitin on a nigga to get bacc so that we can hit the telly for a few hours n get a freak on."* he added as he handed Legend a $50 bill. Legend gladly accepted the money. After putting the bill in his short pockets, he dug into his boxer briefs and took out the two 8ths for Trey.

"Good lookin cuhz; csafe out here n tell the locs I sent my blue passion when they get here." Trey said before walking off in the same that direction he came from. Legend kept his eyes on him all the way until he made the left into East Tremont and he could no longer be seen.

Something wasn't right about Trey and he knew it. *"Wat bithces nigga, we all kno yuh aint got none of them."*

201

Legend thought to himself as he walked inside of Big Homies' Store.

- - -

"Nigga yuh sure that he's the only one out there?" Noni asked his man for the third time. After June was gunned down, Noni didn't know what else to do. To him, it seem like his men were getting knocked off one by one and he knew deep down inside that someday, he would be next. Therefore, he made up his mind not to sit around and wait, but to make the first move.

"Yeah that nigga solo n he out there like he aint got no care in the world." Noni's man shot back. *"Oh, okay copy! Say no more I'm about to go see watssup with that nigga scrap, good lookin out cuhz!"* Noni said giving his man some dap before he got out of his car. Shortly after, he pulled off.

- - -

Legend got another pack of fronto and papers before he walked out of Big Homies' store. Today was every pot head's day and Legend was going to make sure that he smoked until he passed out. On his way to his building he felt like someone was watching him.

202

Legend looked around in suspicion, but was not able to spot anything out of place; so he continued to make his way into his building. When he entered the building, he made his way in the direction of his apartment, but before he was able to put the key in the key hole he felt a metal object pressed to the back of his head.

"Dont even think about it," the voice said from behind him. *"Open the door n dont do nothin stupid or I'm gon leave yuh right where yuh stand."* the voice from behind him added. The only thing that was going through Legend's mind at the time was how the hell did he get caught lacking after his gut feeling was telling him something was off since the moment he woke up that morning.

Although Legend hadn't seen the gun man's face, deep down inside he knew who it was without having to turn around and look into his face. Without wasting any time, he did as he was instructed; he felt like when they entered his apartment, that he would have a better chance of surviving.

The gun man pushed him inside of his apartment a soon as the door was opened completely. Once in the apartment, the gun man led Legend into his room. *"Nigga, yuh really got some balls comin over like yuh runnin shit."* Legend said.

203

"Nigga shut the fuck up!" the gun man said, crashing the butt of his gun to the back of Legend's head causing him to fall to his knees. Blood started pouring immediately from the fresh wound. *"Ya bitch ass aint in no position to be talkin crazy nigga."* the gun man added.

"Come on Noni, yuh gone kill me n wat yuh think my mans is goin to come bacc n do to yuh? Or do yuh really think yuh can get away with this shit?" Legend retorted, still holding the back of his head. *"Yuh might as well kill me n get gone bcos if yuh get caught in here, ya ass is grass!"* he added.

Not likin Legend's last comment and tired of the back and forth, Noni raised his .40 cal to the back of Legend's head and fired.

BOOM!

BOOM!

BOOM!

The three shots killed Legend instantly in execution style. Blood and brain matters splattered all over Noni's face and clothes; using his left hand, he wiped his face, stepping over Legend's dead corpse. Noni started ransacking the little apartment.

After only a few minutes of looking around, he found everything he was looking for. On his way out of the apartment, he gave Legend the 'is he dead' kick. *"Bitch ass nigga!"* he said before walking out of the apartment.

- - -

Detective Gonsalez sat on his desk looking over a few of the unsolved murder files when the call came through the dispatcher. *"Attention all units, shot fired on 178st! I repeat shots fired on 178st! All units please report to the scene."*

Hearing this caused Detective Gonsalez to stop what he was doing; he got up from his desk, grabbed his flight jacket and headed out through his office's door. *"Hold on, wait on me!"* Detective Rosario tried to say, but his partner was already long gone and out of the door.

Wasting no time, Detective Rosario got up from his desk and chased behind his partner. He knew that they don't have no business going where they were about to go, but he wasn't going to let his partner go into this all alone.

It took the two detectives seven minutes in total to reach the crime scene. When they got there, the ambulance and a few unmarked cars were already on the scene. Parking their squad car on the corner of 178st and Author Avenue, the two detectives exited the car.

"Why are yuh guys standing out here?" Detective Rosario was the first to ask as they reached the three detectives that were standing in front of the building 620. "Because we are not allowed inside, the FBI is in there n they dont want no detectives interfering with their investigations." one of the detectives said. Hearing this made Detective Gonsalez turn beat red in the face.

"So yuh tellin me that we cant fuckin take care of our own issues around here, the last time I checked this was our jurisdiction!" Detective Gonsalez shot back. *"That's exactly how they makin it seem detective."* the other detective retorted.

Detective Gonsalez took a deep breath. One thing he didn't tolerate was disrespect, no matter who it came from, hi-ups or not. *"Do yuh guys at least kno wat happened in there?"* Detective Rosario asked. *"From what we heard, someone that went by the name Legend was shot and killed execution style in his own apartment."* the detective replied.

Detective Gonsalez couldn't believe what he had just heard the detective say. He knew Legend very well. He was a suspect on one of his murders cases. Without saying another word, Detective Gonsalez walked away from the scene in the direction of his unmarked car with Detectvie Rosario not too far behind.

Chapter Thirty-Eight

After dropping his son of to his mother in Clinton Towers, Boo navigated his truck up 179th street. When he reached the corner, he turned left into Hughes Avenue. *"Wat the fucc happened here?"* Boo said to himself as he spotted the fleet of Police cars parked throughout the block.

Being that he was riding dirty, Boo didn't want to back out of the block to avoid any unwanted attention. Double parking the X5 he was driving, Boo hopped out the truck and started to make his way to the corner of 178st; his heart skipped a beat when he spotted the gang of Police walking in and out of Legend's building.

Looking around the crowd of people, he spotted a familiar face; he recognized a girl by name of Justine. *"Hey watssup Justine, wat the hell happened here?"* Boo asked when he got close enough to Justine.

"OMG Boo! Yuh aint gon believe this. They killed Legend, someone went into his house n killed him in cold blood!" Justine said. After hearing that Legend had been killed, Boo zoned out not being able to hear anything else that Justine was saying.

"Boo! Boo! Are yuh even listenin to me?" Justine added, snapping Boo out of his train of thoughts. Not even for one minute did he want to believe that his main man was

gone; but he knew that there was a strong possibility that he was.

"Yes I'm listenin to yuh Justine, I'm just tryin to process everythin yuh tellin me." Boo responded trying to stop the tear from falling. *"How the hell did this happen, I just spoke to my nigga."* Boo thought to himself; but what he said out loud was different. *"Was anybody caught on the scene?"* he asked Justine.

"No, they goin around askin question to see if anyone seen or heard something but everyone is claimin that they didnt hear anything" Justine said. "Damn! Okay look, I need yuh to do me a favor n sit tight until every cop car leaves the blocc. If yuh happen to hear anythin please give me a call." Boo finally said giving Justine his number.

"Ok, I sure will; dont worry i got yuh." Justine replied. Justine always had a crush on Boo, but Boo never seem to pay her no mind. Justine was a bad bitch but she just wasn't Boo's type. Without any further words, Boo started making his way back to his truck.

BOOM! BOOM! BOOM! Boo punch the steering wheel as hard as he could, frustrated as the tears that he was trying to fight away finally escaped his eyes and rolled down his cheeks. *"Damn my nigga, how yuh get caught slippin like this, this aint yuh loco."* Boo thought to himself; after getting himself together Boo put his truck in gear and reversed all the way until he hit the corner of 180th.

"Dont worry cuhz i kno who's behind this, n I'm gon make sure that he get the same treatment he gave yuh, if not worse." Boo promised his fallen soldier while he navigated his truck in the direction of True Blue's apartment to relate the news about Legend to him face to face.

Chapter Thirty-Nine

"Hello!" Capo said into the receiver. It was Reddot. *"Capo, wats craccin cuhz? Talk to me nice my guy."* Reddot responded. *"Aint shit loco here; about to leave the Telly right now, why wassup?"* Capo shot back. *"Oh nah! I just wanted to see where yuh was at, bcos I'm gon need yuh to stop on Belmont n collect that bread from Cavs for me. I'm in for the night loco n plus yuh got my car nigga."* Reddot said.

Earlier on that day, Capo had asked Reddot to use his car while he went to go meet up with his little side chick. To avoid anyone saying that they spotted his car in a motel's parking lot, Capo decided to ask Reddot for his car in which he agreed.

"That shit ain't about nothin loco, I'll do that shit for yuh. Just make sure that them niggas got everythin ready for when I get there loco." capo retorted jumping into Reddot's car. *"Aight copy cuhz, let me get off this line so that I can call them niggas."* Reddot shot back. *"Aight bet, say no more loco."* Capo said before ending the call.

A few minutes passed when a text from Reddot came through his phone. *'Loco them niggas waitin on yuh right now, let me kno when yuh out front loco.'* the text from Reddot read. Putting his phone back into the cup holder,

Capo put the car in gear and pulled off out of the Crown Motor inn's parking lot.

- - -

– Meanwhile … –

'Yo fatboii, I'm on my way to go collect that bread, have that shit ready for when I get there nigga!' Cavs just looked at his phone screen as he re-read Reddot's message. *"Don't worry nigga I got ya bread plus somethin extra."* Cavs thought to himself. Cavs has been waiting all week for this opportunity and today the break he's been looking for all week finally came. *'Aight nigga.'* Cavs texted back.

"Wats that nigga talkin about tribu?" C-Lite asked. *"That nigga said that he's on his way right now. So ya tu save tribu."* Cavs shot back with a smile on his face. Cavs was tired of Reddot disrespecting him every chance he got and tonight he planned on making him pay for the disrespect.

"Copy, say no more then tribu." C-Lite shot back. Cavs and C-Lite sat inside their trap, both strapped with Glock .40s patiently waiting on Reddot's arrival.

- - -

By the time capo reach the corner of Belmont Avenue, it was 11:45pm. Pulling up to the front of Cavs' building he parked. Taking his phone from the cup holder he sent Reddot another

211

text. A few seconds passed before another text came through from Reddot. Anuel AA's 'Ayer' played out of the car speakers.

Capo adjusted himself to get comfortable in the leather seats, smoking a blunt of kush as he waited for Cavs. *'Yo fatboii, I'm down stairs nigga, hurry ya ass up!'* Cavs read the message from Reddot; a smile spread across his face. *"Come on tribu, that bitch ass nigga down stairs."* Cavs turned and said to C-Lite.

'CLICK! CLOCK!' After making sure that their weapons were locked and loaded. They made their way out of the apartment. *"Look tribu, once we get to that window we lettin that bitch nigga have it. Yuh kno how he play so we cant take no chances."* Cavs said to C-Lite before they exited the building and made their way towards Reddot's car.

As they approached the car with only a few feet away, all hell broke loose as Cavs and C-Lite raised their guns and started filling Reddot's car with lead; making it rock back and forth. *BOOM! BOOM! BOOM! BOC! BOC! BOOM! BOC! BOOM! BOC! BOC!*

Cap had no chance as the bullets from the powerful weapons pierced through his upper body and face. Luckily, the first three bullets had struck him dead in his face killing him instantly. Cavs and C-Lite didn't let up until both of their guns had kicked back empty.

"Bitch ass nigga! How yuh like those apples!" Cavs finally said, while throwing the brown paper bag through the broken driver side window. *"Yuh can take that with yuh where ever yuh goin nigga."* he added.

Throwing their hoodies over their head, Cavs and C-Lite walked off in the same direction they had come from with no care in the word. Now that Reddot was gone, Cavs felt like the load he's been carrying for over a year had finally been lifted off his shoulders.

"We got his bitch ass tribu!" C-Lite said excitedly. *"Yeah I kno, I told yuh that, that nigga wasn't untouchable tribu. That nigga bleed just like we bleed."* Cavs shot back, lighting the half of blunt of weed that rested in the ash tray.

- - -

– Meanwhile ... –

Reddot sat on his couch dumbfounded; he couldn't believe what he had just heard the News Reporter say. *"Damn Capo!"* Reddot said to himself. *"That dead could have been me, was that hit meant for me?"* Reddot asked himself. Not too long after the thought crossed his mind Reddot knew that it could have only been one nigga behind all this – Cavs.

213

"That nigga probably thought that was me inside my car and tried to take me out." Reddot said trying to put two and two together. Right there and then he decided to make Cavs pay for the stunt he had just pulled off. The only thing he needed to figure out was who the other shooter that was with him was; but that wouldn't be that hard to find out.

Shutting the TV off, Reddot got up from his couch and made his way toward his room, where Shawny laid peacefully asleep on his king sized bed. *"Damn Capo."* was all Reddot kept saying to himself. For some reason, Reddot felt like it was his fault that Capo had gotten killed.

- - -

Lou-Lou was sitting on her fire escape like she did every night before going bed, smoking on a blunt of loud when out of nowhere all hell broke loose right under her fire escape; causing her to drop her freshly rolled blunt down the fire escape. Lou-Lou couldn't believe what she was witnessing as she watched Cavs and C-Lite standing side by side shooting into the car that was parked in front of her building.

Lou-Lou watched the whole scene unfold right in front of her. Lou-Lou laid in her bed that night and after four hours of tussling and turning; she was finally able to find her sleep. What she had just witnessed had her scared, she had seen dead bodies before, but she had never witnessed someone actually commit murder until now.

Chapter Forty

True Blue walked out of the Bronx Supreme Court with a 'cool aid' smile on his face. Although he's been sentenced to serve 2 to 4 years in State prison, he wasn't going to allow anything to knock off his cloud. A few hours prior, on April 24th, 2017 at around 1:35am 'IVAN ANDY ACOSTA' was born. Due to that fact alone, the judge had granted a three months extension before he had to turn himself in.

Walking across the street into the mall's parking lot, True Blue made his way in the direction in where his S550 was parked. Jumping in the drivers' seat, he hit the push start botton, bringing the car to life. Putting it in gear, he pulled out of the mall's parking lot.

Ten minutes later, True Blue was pulling up to the Bronx Leburnard Hospital. After finding a parking spot around the corner from the Hospital, True Blue made his way into the hospital. Jumping in the elevator, he made his way up to the 4th floor where Aisha's room was located.

"Hey! How are my babies feelin this morning?" True Blue said as he walked into Aisha's room. Aisha was sitting up on her hospital bed feeding Ivan a bottle of milk. True Blue walked over to them and gave the both of them a kiss in their cheeks.

"Watssup lil man?" True Blue said to his twin. Ivan was a split image of True Blue. Looking at Ivan was like looking directly into True Blue's eyes, there was no denying that was his son, and he wouldn't have wanted it any other way.

"Hey babe, how was court?" Aisha finally said when True Blue had taken a seat on the chair that was right by her bed. *"Court was okay babe."* True Blue quickly said. *"Can I feed him ma?"* he then asked trying to change the subject before their moment was spoilt with bad news.

Aisha sensed that something was wrong but decided to not say anything at the moment. *"Of course yuh can my love, wat kind of question is that?"* Aisha said while handing Lil IV to his father.

"Watssup lil man, I see yuh a lil hungry this mornin huh?" True Blue said to his twin. He could tell that Lil IV was hungry from the way that he was sucking on the bottles nipple. *"Yuh kno I love yuh right? Yuh the best thing that has ever happen to me lil man. Yuh are my pride n joy never forget that, okay?"* he added while still looking directly into Ivan's eyes who was also looking back at him as if he understood everything his father was saying.

Aisha sat on the bed admiring her two favorite men in the world. From the way True Blue talked to his son and the way he carried him, there was no doubt in Aisha's mind that he would be a great father to their son.

"Watssup babe, why yuh lookin at me like that?" True Blue asked, after looking up and seeing that Aisha was staring at him. *"Nothin babe, I just love this view, I love the way yuh are with him n he hasn't even been in this world a full 24 hours yet. I can tell that yuh goin to be a great father to him n I love that about yuh babe."* Aisha said, as her eyes got teary.

"Awww babe, thank yuh. But yuh don't have to cry ma bcos yuh gon have a nigga here cryin right with yuh!" True Blue said and they both laughed. *"Babe, do yuh think he knows who I am?"* True Blue asked, as he place Lil IV over his shoulders so that he could begin to burp him. *"Of course, he know yuh his daddy babe, he remembers your voice from when yuh used to speak to him in my belly. He remembers very well babe."* Aisha assured him.

True Blue ended up staying at the hospital with his family until the visiting hours were over. When the time came for him to say his goodbyes, his eyes got all watery. Leaving his family behind was something that he wasn't too happy about, even though it was only temporary.

"Awwn, babe dont cry." Aisha said noticing the tears in True Blue's eyes. *"Yuh kno that yuh can come back*

tomorrow bright n early my love." Aisha said giving True Blue a kiss on his lips.

"*Yeah, I kno but I just wish that I could take y'all home today with me.*" True Blue stated giving Lil IV a kiss on his four head. After he finished saying his goodbyes, True Blue walked out of Aisha's room with plans to return the next morning.

- - -

– A Couple of Days Later –

Today was the day that True Blue had been waiting for. Today was the day that Aisha and his lil man would finally get discharged from the hospital. After making sure that the house was clean to a 'T', True Blue went and jumped in the shower. Thirty minutes later, he was dressed and out the door on his way to the hospital.

Chapter Forty-One

Lil Rico cruised through the Mena streets of the South Bronx with no set destination. Driving around with no set destination was something he did whenever he had something weighing heavy on his mind. Dave East bumped out of the Chrysler's speakers. The spell of weed was heavy in the car.

A week has passed since Legend's funeral, due to the fact that he was shot twice in the back of his head, they were forced to send him away in a closed casket with none of them being able to see their fallen soldier one last time. Things haven't been the same since Legend's murder.

Today was Capo's funeral, but no one knew where it was taking place; his mother doesn't want any of them to attend the funeral. To her, it was their fault as to why her son was no longer with her. Although they weren't allowed to go the funeral, that didn't stop them from making sure that they took care of the funeral's bill.

"Where did we go wrong?" Lil Rico thought to himself as he made the left turn on Southern Boulevard. He couldn't believe how things were just starting to look up for them and in a blink of an eye everything seemed to be spiraling out of control. Everything that Lil Rico and True Blue worked so hard for was starting to crumble.

220

Lil Rico stopped reporting to parole; there was no doubts in his mind that he now he had a warrant out for his arrest. Being that he wasn't too far from Mike's block, he decided to stop by and make sure that everything was running smooth. Five minute later, Lil Rico was pulling up in front of Mike's building.

"Yo Mike, wats craccin cuhz, I'm out front pulling up." Lil Rico said into the receiver when mike answered. *"Copy loco, say no more. I'm coming down stairs right now."* Mike shot back before ending the call. A few seconds later Mike finally made his way out of his building and walked in the direction of Lil Rico's car.

"Wats the word big bro! Wat yuh doin in these parts, the money wont be ready till Friday." Mike said once he was in the car. *"Yeah, I kno loco, that's not why I'm here cuhz. I was in the area so i decided to stop by n make sure that yuh was good over here loco."* Lil Rico said lighting the blunt of loud he just had finished rolling.

"Oh, okay copy my guy. Shit all good on this end tho. Yuh kno I got shit under control loco; aint nothin movin unless I say so!" Mike responded taking the blunt Lil Rico was passing him.

Lil Rico and Mike smoked four blunts in total before Lil Rico decided that it was time for him to roll. After saying

221

their goodbyes, Lil Rico put the Chrysler in gear and pulled away from Mike's building. *"Just cause y'all gone dont mean that y'all would ever be forgotten. As long as we still walking this bitch, y'all names would forever be remembered."* Lil Rico said to himself.

- - -

– Meanwhile ... –

"Nigga, I told ya scary ass that we was good tribu! Them niggas beefin with so many niggas that they dont even know where the shit came from!" Cavs bragged as he, C-Lite and Montana sat in their trap smoking on some new yorks finest. *"That nigga Reddot still come through here like shit all peaches n cream nigga!"* he added giving C-Lite some dap.

"Yeah I aint gon lie, I thought they was going to find out. I'm glad they didn't tho; bcos who knows how shit would have turned out right now or where we would have been right now." C-Lite said, already knowing how True Blue and his crew got down.

Montana sat off to the side without saying a word. The block has been hot since Capo's murder; but things were starting to get better as the time went on. The money was starting to roll in once again and they couldn't have wanted it any other way.

- - -

"Damn Lou-Lou, yuh act like yuh aint tryin to fucc wit a nigga ma?" Remo said once he spotted the Dominican beauty that lived on the 5th floor walked into the building. *"Remo, it's not that. It's that I kno how ya baby moma is n I dont want any problems. If it wasn't because of her I would've let yuh beat this pussy up."* Lou-Lou responded.

Lou-Lou also had a thing for Remo, but due to the fact that he had a baby mama that played no games when it came to him, she decided to keep her distance to avoid any confrontations with her.

"But who said that my CM gonna kno about wat we got goin on?" Remo said. *"Shit I dont kiss n tell and if I'm not mistakin, I kno yuh aint doin no kiss n tellin?"* Remo added. By now Remo and Lou-Lou had started walking in the direction of the elevators.

Lou-Lou had on a pair of black Spendex with a white see through blouse, she wore no bra and her nipples were poking through the fabric. Lou-Lou resembles the love hip-hop reality star – April without the chinky eyes. The elevator doors finally opened and Lou-Lou stepped inside.

"I was just about to go upstairs n face these two blunts, yuh trying to smoke then?" Lou-Lou asked *"I mean I*

223

aint doin nothin right now ma. I got something to match ya two blunts." Remo shot back.

"Cool, so come on lets go to my place because yuh kno how nosy these people in this buildin are." Lou-Lou retorted wasting no time, Remo stepped in the elevator and he Lou-Lou rode the elevator together to the 5th floor.

Chapter Forty-Two

– RIGHT BACC –

Becoming a father was the best thing that ever happened for True Blue; he loved every minute of it. Lil Ivan had brought so much joy into their home and things couldn't have been better. Seeing the way Hailey interacted with her little brother was breath taking. She was a big help around the house and was very hands on when it came to helping her mother with her little brother.

With everything that was going on around True Blue, the only place he felt and found peace was at home with his family. True Blue knew that he had one main priority which was taking care of his family and making sure that they didn't need or want for nothing.

True Blue has been dropping music nonstop. His latest single was called 'RIGHT BACC'. The single has only been out three weeks and people were already demanding to see the visual. 'RIGHT BACC' had the streets in frenzy and it was becoming one of the fans' favorite.

Due to the fact that time wasn't on his side, True Blue decided to give his fans what they had all been dying to see – the visual for 'RIGHT BACC'. Rolling out of bed, True Blue walked over to the dresser and grabbed his phone. Signing into his FaceBook page, he began to type;

'TODAY IS THE DAY YALL ALL BEEN WAITIN!!! RIGHT BACC VIDEO SHOOT!

TODAY AT 5PM ON H-BLOCC!

IF YUH CRIP'N PULL UP! ALL 30S MUST SHOW!

#SHMOVIE YUH DONT WANT TO MISS IT!

#LEGENDARYSHIT

#FREEDA9

#MRTOP30HIMSELF!'

That was the message that True Blue just had finished posting; and within seconds, his notifications started going crazy. By the time it had hit 1.00 pm, True Blue's message had already gained 1,500 likes and 700 comments.

After he had showered, True Blue made his lil' man a bottle of warm milk; and after feeding and burping him, True Blue gave his favorite three a kiss on the cheek and promised to see them later before walking out of the door.

Twenty minutes later, True Blue pulled up to the front of Flaco's barbershop on the corner of Belmont Avenue and East Tremont Avenue. Parking his S550 right in front of the shop, he exited the car and made his way into the barbershop. *"Klok!"* True Blue greeted the first two barbers. *"Y Flaco?"* he asked. *"Klok Blue! No Flaco no here today mi brother."* Motherfuccer, one of the barbers said, as he continued to cut the hair of the dude that was on his chair.

"Wat yuh mean he not here, he not comin in today?" True Blue shot back. He couldn't believe that in the day that he need him the most, Flaco had decided to not come around. *"No, he no come in today Blue, took today off."*

226

Motherfuccer replied. Without saying another word, True Blue turned and walked out of the barbershop heated.

Instead of jumping back into his car, he decided to cross the street instead to see if his man JC was working. Reaching the Millionaire's Barbershop, True Blue spotted JC sitting on his chair with a new paper in his hands. Pushing the door open, he stepped inside.

"Oh shit! Look at who we got here! Wats craccin cuhs!" JC said when he spotted True Blue; putting his newspaper down, he got up from his seat and gave True Blue some dap. *"Wat bring yuh to this part of town?"* JC asked nervously fearing the worst. *"Wats craccin old head! How yuh?"* True Blue responded. *"Aint shit cuhz, I have a video shoot tonight n I need yuh to laze my shit up; this nigga Flaco aint come in today."* True Blue added.

"Oh okay okay, Yuh kno I got yuh. Seat down let me get yuh all sharpened up cuhz!." JC stated, feeling a little more at ease. For a second, JC had thought that his hand had been exposed. After letting JC know what kind of hair cut he wanted, JC began to work his magic.

"Watssup how yuh been cuhz, I hear that business been good with yuh n my cuhz." JC asked trying to start some small talk. *"Yeah son good money n a very good business man."* True Blue shot back, not really trying to entertain the conversation. The truth was that True Blue felt like whatever him and Jay had going on wasn't JC's business; cousin or not.

An hour later, JC was putting the finishing touches on True Blue's dark ceaser. *"All done cuhz! Yuh ready to go now!"* JC said turning True Blue around so that he can take a good look at his fresh hair cut in the mirror. After taking a good look at the job JC had done, True Blue reached in his pockets and handed JC a $50 bill.

True Blue dapped him up and thanked him for hooking him up before walking back out of the barbershop. Looking at the time on his bust down Rolex, True Blue noticed that he only had two hours left before the camera man showed up for the video shoot.

- - -

It was 4:30pm and H-BLOCC was packed with all the people that had come out to show True Blue some love. Nothing but blue was all that was seen from blocks away. Gang had showed out and the bitches came out to play wearing the skimpiest outfits they were able to fit in.

The liquor and the smell of weed smoke were heavy in the air. It took five hours to complete the shoot. Thankfully, no issues took place and the shoot was a success. The camera man and the vibe were on point. The only thing True Blue felt like he was missing was his niggas; Legend and Capo. Till this day he still couldn't believe that they were gone. Not being in a position to drive, True Blue had Aisha come pick him up at around 2.00 am.

- - -

After the video shoot was over, Lil Rico made his way to his car with two Dominican and black beauties. The plan was to take the party to the nearest hotel. Jenifer and Jessica were from, New Jersey and after seeing True Blue's post on FaceBook, the sisters decided to attend the event.

After the movie that they had just witnessed, they were happy that they did come. Jenifer favored the actress Jessica Alba while Jessica favored the Latina singer Demi Levato. Lighting the blunt he had just finished rolling, Lil Rico pulled the Chrysler into traffic.

True Blue's single 'RIGHT BACC' played out the car speakers. *"Fucc!"* Lil Rico said, after noticing that he had just hit the red light. Not too long after Lil Rico hit the light, a black on black unmarked car pulled up behind him and turned on its flashing lights. *"Pull the car over!"* the detectives inside of the unmarked car said through the bull's horn.

Not wanting to cause any unwanted drama, Lil Rico decided to pull over. He knew that deep down inside, nothing good was going to come out of this. Lil Rico pulled over and parked right in front of the Little Ceaser's Pizza shop. Looking in the rear view mirror, Lil Rico shook his head as he spotted the two detectives step out of the unmarked car.

Not only was he riding dirty, but he knew that deep down inside, there was a parole warrant out for his arrest. Lil Rico thought about taking off and taking the two detectives on a high speed chase; but as soon as the thought came to mind it left. He didn't want to put his new female friends in any danger.

- - -

– Meanwhile … –

"Thank y'all all for comin out today! IT WAS A FUCCIN SHMOVIE!! #LEGENDARYSHIT!" True Blue re-read his post before he actually posted it on his FaceBook page. Not too long after the post was uploaded to his FaceBook page, his phone started going off with an unknown number. *"Who the fucc is this?"* True Blue thought to himself. He normally doesn't take any unknown numbers but for some reasons, something told him that he should take this one.

"Hello!" True Blue said into the receiver. *"Hey, hello is this True Blue?"* the voice on the other end asked. *"Yeah who's this?"* True Blue shot back, wondering who was calling his phone at that time of the night.

"Sorry for callin yuh so late my name is Jessica, but I just wanted to call yuh n let yuh kno that your brother just got locked up. We was on our way to a hotel when they pulled his car over n after searchin it, they found a loaded weapon." Jessica said. True Blue couldn't believe what the female named Jessica had just said. To him it felt like his world was crashing down behind him. The only thing that was normal around him was his family.

230

"Damn smh, thank yuh for callin me Jessica, there's nothin we can do at the moment but first thin in the morning, I'm goin to make sure I find out wats really goin on okay? Thank yuh n if yuh like I'll keep yuh posted." True Blue finally said, still not believing that his brother had just gotten picked up. With everything that has been going on, True Blue immediately started fearing the worst.

"Yes, please do, n if he calls yuh please give him my number, I'm goin to text yuh from it now." Jessica said before ending the call. Once off the phone True Blue placed his phone back on the dresser. Walking over to the bed, he got in the bed with Aisha and Lil Ivan.

"Wat happened babe, who was that?" Aisha asked when True Blue was completely in bed. *"That was some girl named Jessica, she was callin me to let me kno that AL just got locced up."* True Blue explained. *"Oh my gawd, babe wat happened?"* Aisha shot back in a low calm tone, trying not to wake Lil Ivan up.

"I dont kno all the details yet babe, but she said that they found a gun in the car when he was pulled over a lil' while ago." True Blue said. Not wanting to put any more pressure on her man, Aisha decided to drop the subject for the time being.

"Well, just take it easy babe n try to get some rest. When we wake up later, we would find out wats goin on with AL." Aisha stated, giving her man a kiss on the lips. *"Yuh have a point there my love, plus I aint even gon lie, I'm tired*

231

as hell right now. The video was successful but I'll fill yuh on later on today about how everythin went." True Blue said. *"Okay babe."* was all Aisha said before she drifted off back to sleep. An hour later, True Blue was right behind her.

Chapter Forty-Three

"Damn Yari, wat yuh tryin to do to a nigga?" Lefty said in between moans. The way Yari was sucking his dick was driving him crazy, to the point in where his toes was curling up while his eyes rolled to the back of his head. The spitting and the slurping sounds that she was making in the process wasn't making it any better.

Lefty never fucked none of his hoes, a blow job here and there was about as far as he went. Lefty, Mariah and Yari had been at the El Rancho motel for the past 48 hours. The El Rancho motel was located in the Gunhill section of the Bronx. While Mariah was out on an out call, Lefty had decided to get a nut off.

In the 48 hours that he has been in the small motel room, he had already made a little over $8,600; with Yari bringing in the majority of the money. *"Daddy, cum in my mouch pleaseee."* Yari moaned as she glided Lefty's dick in and out of her mouth.

"Thats wat yuh want daddy to do?" Lefty replied, ready to release his load. *"Mmmhhmm,"* Yari mumbled while she held Lefty's dick in her mouth. A few seconds afterwards, Lefty finally gave Yari exactly what she was asking for and came all in her mouth.

"Aaaggghhh!" Lefty moaned as Yari sucked off every drop out of him. After making sure she had gotten every drop, Yari got up of the bed and walked in the direction of the bathroom. After she finished brushing her

233

teeth and washing her face, Yari walked back out of the bathroom, walking over to the bed she sat on it.

Lefty was on the other side of the bed smoking on the blunt he had just finished rolling. 'Knock Knock!' There was a knock on the door. *"Ma, that must be Mariah, can yuh go let her in for me."* Lefty said when he heard the knocking on the motel room's door. Without saying a word, Yari got up of the bed and went to go do as she was told.

"Hey Boo how was ya day?" Yari asked Mariah as soon as she opened the door. *"Hey bitch! My day was okay, wat can I say? I just made $350 for a lil' conversation. The nigga's dick couldn't even get hard and when it finally did, that nigga's time was up!"* Mariah narrated stepping into the motel room.

Wasting no time Mariah walked over to the side of the bed where Lefty was laying; reaching in her hand bag she pulled out the $350 and handed it over to Lefty. *"It's all there daddy daddy ..."*

"Good!" was all that Lefty was able to say before the door to the motel's room was kicked opened *"D.E.A! Don't nobody move! Everybody get the fuck on the ground now!"* The lead agent said as he stepped into the motel's room.

Lefty couldn't believe what was happening let alone why it was happening. Before he knew it, he was tackled to the ground and so were Mariah and Yari. *"Wat the fucc is goin on?"* was all that Lefty kept asking himself as he was placed in handcuffs. After being cuffed, Lefty was led out of the motel's room by three D.E.A agents.

"I hope these bitches don't throw me under the buss." Lefty thought to himself as he was placed inside of the unmarked car. Two minutes later, Mariah and Yari were also escorted out of the motel's room in cuffs and placed into two different unmarked cars.

- - -

– Four Hours Later –

Lefty has been in the interrogation room for the past four hours. After seeing that he wasn't willing to cooperate, the lead agent stormed out of the room leaving Lefty without a t-shirt in the cold room in hopes that he would break and give in.

Hearing the interrogation room door open, Lefty raised his head up off the metal table. *"Since yuh wanted to play hard ball, then we decided to play hard ball right alone with yuh Mr. Rodriguez."* Agent Gomez started to say closing the door behind him. *"Not only are yuh bein charged with human tracffickin, yuh are also bein Booked on a parole violation as well. So with ya record, yuh lookin at anything between 5 years to 20 years in prison."* Agent Gomez continued.

Lefty was placed back in handcuffs and was escorted out of the interrogation room. On his way out of the interrogation room, Lefty passed one of the holding cells,

235

looking inside of the bull pen he spotted Mariah sitting in the far end of the cell, Yari was nowhere in sight.

The whole time, Lefty was trying to make eye contact with Mariah, but for some reason, Mariah wasn't trying to make any eye contact with him. *"Damn!"* was all Lefty kept saying to himself as he was escorted out of the 48th Precinct. *"I hope these bitches aint sell me out ..."* he thought to himself.

Chapter Forty-Four

It's been three months since Legend and Capo were killed; and now that Lefty and Lil Rico were locked up, Boo was one of the only few ones on H-Blocc. Being that True Blue had a new responsibility, his time on the block was limited.

Alone or not, Boo didn't seem to mind, as long as the money was rolling in. Reddot on the other hand was still laying low in the Pink Houses Projects in the East New York section of Brooklyn; only showing his face in the Bronx when it was necessary.

For the past few days, Boo has been having a funny feeling that he was being watched; and after being followed to his mother's house a few days prior by a black on black charger, he needed no further proof. Right there and then he knew that something wasn't adding up.

As Boo stood in front of Big Homie's Deli grocery store, he looked down the block to 179th street and spotted the same black charger that was following him the other day; his heart started beating faster in his chest. *"Wat the fucc, are these mutherfuccer the Feds."* Boo thought to himself.

Not wanting to stick around any longer, Boo decided to call it a night. Walking over to where his X5 was parked at, Boo jumped in and pushed the start botton to bring the truck to life. Pulling out of the parking space, Boo navigated the foreign car into traffic.

Looking in the rear view mirror, just like he expected the black charger was only three cars behind him. *"Damn these niggas on a nigga's dicc."* Boo said to himself as he thought about a perfect plan to shake the jakes.

- - -

– Meanwhile … –

"Damn ma, I dead love ya accent, that shit be makin a nigga dicc jump in my pants." Remo said into the receiver. He was on the phone with Lou Lou. *"Oh yeah, thats wat I do to ju pa'?"* Lou Lou replied in the sexiest voice that she could muster. *"Damn sure do ma, yuh need to hurry ya ass bacc up here bcos daddy miss his pussy."* Remo shot back.

"Mmm, I aint even gon lie. I dead miss tha big black dick too daddy. Just thinkin about the way yuh be fuckin me, my pussy gettin wet." Lou Lou said almost in a moan; but being that she had left to D.R. a few days prior, there was really nothing they could do other than to wait until she returned to put out the fire that they were both feeling.

"Dont worry papi, I'll be back up there sometime next week n when I do, I'm gon need yuh to punish this pussy." Lou Lou stated. *"Oh yuh aint gotta worry about that ma, because I plan on doin just that!"* Remo responded, gripping his dick through his G-star jeans.

"Not to change the subject ma, but wat was it that yuh had to tell me before yuh left to D.R.?" Remo asked, remembering that Lou Lou had told him that she had something to tell him before leaving for D.R.

238

"Oh that, yuh gon have to wait until I get back pa'. Some things are not for the phone; and wat I have to tell yuh is one of those things." Lou Lou shot back. *"Lou Lou!"* Remo heard someone yell on the other end of the phone. *"Pa let me let yuh go, I'll call yuh again tomorrow. Let me go see wat my grandma needs help with now."* Lou Lou added. Before Remo was able to reply, Lou Lou had already ended the call. *"Damn, that was rude."* Remo said looking at his phone.

Shortly after, Remo placed his phone on the couch; the front door to his apartment had opened and in came his baby mother and his three kids. *"Oh shit I need to tighten up."* Remo said to himself, as the thought of almost getting caught talking to another female crossed his mind.

To play it off as if he wasn't on his phone, Remo quickly reached over to the small coffee table, grabbing the half of blunt off the ash tray and lit it before the mother of his kids was able to make it to the living room.

Chapter Forty-Five

"Good afternoon! Ladies and gentlemen." The chief of the FBI said as he stepped on the podium, greeting every agent in attendance. *"Okay, so I brought you all here today to fill you guys in on where we are today with the Hughes Avenue crew. As we already know, we are not dealing with some average street dealers; these individuals are not to be taken lightly. These two individuals are who we believe to be the leaders of the Hughes crew."*

The chief paused for a brief second as he pointed at the bulletin board on the wall with Lil Rico's and True Blue's picture. *"Both of these individuals both have a mile long criminal history. Robberies, drugs, guns, attempted murders are what their records consist of, to name a few. Our field agents Rodriguez and Weaver have already done a wonderful job in getting all the intel that we needed to bring this case in front of a judge. Thanks to their amazing work; it's the reason why the judge was willing to grant us the warrant to each of these individuals arrest."*

The FBI chief further stated that *"With that being said, the next time we meet in this room, it would be the day that we would be making our move! All members named in this seven man indictment are members of the 'Rollin 30s' set of the nationwide Crips street gang. Mr. Acosta and Mr. Valdez are two high ranks in this organization. So again, take every precaution when taking these individuals into custody. Thank you all for coming, hope you guys continue to enjoy the rest of ya day!"*

Without saying another word, the chief of the FBI stepped down from the podium and made his way out of the conference room. Santana, the chief of the FBI knew that he couldn't afford to make any mistakes and he didn't plan on making one. Making sure that all his 'i(s)' were dotted and all his 't(s)' were crossed was his main and only priority.

Chapter Forty-Six

– BROOKLYN NY –

Reddot had been laying low for the past three weeks in the Pink Houses Projects in the East New York section of Brooklyn at his uncle's house. Things in Castle Hill had heated up after the two bodies dropped, so to be on the safe side Reddot decided to stay away from town for the time being.

Instead of getting his car fixed after Capo's murder, Reddot had decided that it would have been best if he had just copped himself some new wheels and that he did. Reddot drove an X5 straight out of the lot; the same year as Boo's X5, but unlike Boo's; Reddot's X5 was matted black with the peanut butter interior and two 13 inch TVs on the back of the head rest of the driver's and passenger's seats.

The way Capo was murdered was still weighing heavy on Reddot's mind. For some reason, deep down inside, he felt like Cavs was behind Capo's murder and that the only reason Capo was murdered was because he was driving his car at the time. *"That shit was really meant for me."* Reddot constantly thought to himself.

In the mood for some pussy, Reddot decided to give his new flame, Shawny a call. Shawny was the true definition of a bad 'bitch'; she was a student by day and a stripper at one of New York's most lit night club 'Starletts' at night.

- - -

– Fortgreene Projects, BK –

After killing Legend in cold blood, Noni felt that he has no business left in the Bronx; getting revenge for his man June was all that he wanted and once he had gotten it, he wasted no time migrating to Brooklyn. He wasn't a dummy; he knew that True Blue and his crew would be looking for him for the stunt he had pulled off and being a sitting duck wasn't an option.

Noni left out of Legend's crib the day of the murder with 10 pounds of some grand daddy kush and a little over $43,000 in cash. His new found merchandize was enough for him to get on his feet and open up shop in the Fortgreene Projects in Brooklyn NY.

For the past three years, Noni been messing with a female from Brooklyn named Asia. What started out to be just a Booty call from time to time had turned out to be a committed relationship between the two. Asia was head over heels for Noni; she had been trying to get Noni to come live with her since the second month of them talking, but Noni always declined and often told her that when the time was right that they would cross that bridge.

So, with no place else to go, Noni decided to take his talents to Brooklyn and move in with Asia. It's been four months since he and Asia had been living together and Noni already had her Project in a frenzy with the weed. Once Noni

243

opened up shop, it didn't take longer than a week for the word to spread that he had the best weed in the Project.

"Asia, can yuh come here please ma!" Noni shouted in the direction of the back room where he and Asia slept. A few seconds later, Asia came walking into the living room with nothing on but a pair of red boy shorts and a white tank top without a bra, her nipples were poking out of the fabric. Asia resembles the straight stunting magazine model Ms. Cat to a 'T'.

"Watssup pa'?" Asia said standing directly in front of Noni with her camel toe right in his face. *"Babe, why dont yuh come n kneel between these legs n show daddy how much yuh love him."* Noni said. Asia's head game, from a one to ten was on a hundred; super head ain't got nothing on her and her pussy was just the icing on the cake.

Noni loved everything about her and though he often cheated on her, he didn't have any intensions on letting her go. Without saying a word, Asia got on her knees right between Noni's legs. After releasing his semi hard dick out of his basketball short, she licked the tip before slowly taking it into her warm mouth.

"Damn ma, do that thing for daddy." Noni let out a moan. Asia ended up sucking on Noni's dick until her jaw locked and he came all in her mouth. After sucking him dry, she continued to suck on his dick until it came back to life.

Once Noni's dick was nice and hard again, Asia got up from the squatting position she was in, removed her boy shorts, climbed on top of Noni's legs and slowly began to enter his dick into her soaked wet pussy.

"Oooohhhhh! Daaddy! I looovveee this dick!" Asia let out a moan, loving the way Noni's dick filled her up. Noni and Asia ended fucking until they had both cum back to back and passed out right there on the living room couch.

"Eewww! Y'all two mutherfuckers need to take that shit in y'all fuckin room! Don't nobody want to see ya lil ass dick n yuh hoe stink ass pussy!" Shanwy said when she stepped into the apartment and spotted her sister and her man lying ass naked on the living room couch.

It was 2.00 am and Shawny had just got back from a long night of shaking her ass. Shawny was a dime from head to toe; she favored the actress Stacy Dash without the blue eyes. Getting home at 2.00 am was the norm for her since her occupation was stripping. walking pass her sister and her man, Shawny made her way in the direction of her room, when she entered her room, she slammed the room's door behind her.

"Nasty ass nigga!" Shawny thought to herself as she began to undress so she could jump in the shower. Shawny didn't like her sister's man at all, she felt like something wasn't right with him and that he was only using her sister to have somewhere to lay his head at.

"Babe wake up, come on lets go in the room before ya sister come back out here trippin with her crazy ass." Noni said as he tried to slightly wake Asia from her sleep.

245

The two retired to their bedroom where they had another round of steamy hot and sweaty sex.

Chapter Forty-Seven

"So tell me Ish, how are things goin with yuh n True Blue now that the baby is finally here?" Amanda asked Aisha. The two were in front of their mom's building enjoying the nice spring weather while also enjoying about six pack of some ice cold coronas.

"Things between us are great! Thanks to God. It's like the baby came into our life n all he did was bring nothin but happyness into our home. I love the way he is with him, I can already tell that he's goin to be an amazin father to our child." Aisha responded as she took a sip out of her corona.

"Awww, that's so cute! I'm happy for y'all for real for real Ish. I wish yuh and True Blue nothin but the best." Amanda shot back. *"Aint he suppose to be turnin himself in, in a couple of months Ish?"* Eileen, her other sister came out of the left field and asked. Aisha looked up to see Eileen coming out of the building with a corona in one hand and her phone in the other. This was the question that Aisha was hoping was never asked.

"Yeah he's suppose be turnin himself in next month on the 5th." Aisha replied with nothing but hurt in her voice. *"But I rather him go in now and get it over with now that the baby is still lil' n he won't even notice him gone."* she added, taking another sip out of her corona. This was the fourth sip she took back to back since Eileen asked the question.

"Damn that sucks!" Amanda finally said. *"It's crazy that now that his music is startin to take off, that he's gon*

247

need to put it on pause while he goes in n do his time." Amanda added. *"Yeah that's crazy because his video for his latest song is goin crazy on social media n on Youtube."* Eileen said.

"Well, is just like my baby said, he's goin to get it RIGHT BACC! This is just minor setback for a major come back!" Aisha finally added, tired and not really wanting to continue to have this conversation with her sisters.

Eileen and Amanda got the hint and dropped the conversation. The three sisters continued to enjoy their company for the rest of the night until it was time to call it a night.

248

Chapter Forty-Eight

"I'll do anythin for yuh babe." Shawny said. *"Damn ma, where the hell did yuh get this weed from? The last time a nigga had somethin this potent was when my Legend was alive."* Reddot said as he took a few more pulls of the blunt that he and Shawny was smoking on, before passing it back to her.

"I took the shit from my sister's man babe, some nigga named Noni. That nigga got over ten pounds at the house. I don't like the nigga thou babe; so every time I get the chance, I pinch his stash." Shawny shot back.

Reddot couldn't believe what he had just heard Shawny say. He didn't believe in coincident and what Shawny said next confirmed that they in fact were talking about the same nigga. *"One night the nigga came to our apartment late at night with two duffle bags asking my sister to spend a few nights with us and my sister being so dick whipped by the nigga, she agreed in a heartbeat to let him stay with us. Two week turned into two months n two months turned into forever. Later on my sister put me on n told me that the reason why he was stayin with us was because he had robbed somebody up in the Bronx n that they were now lookin for his pussy ass."* Shawny added.

Reddot just stood there listening to everything she had to say without saying a word. *"Damn, it's crazy how small this world really is."* Reddot thought to himself as he tried to put the perfect plan together. Right there and then it hit him. *"Ma did yuh really mean wat yuh had said the other night while we was fuccin?"* Reddot finally asked.

Shawny sat on up the bed and looked at Reddot directly in his eyes. *"Mean wat babe?"* Shawny queried. *"Yuh had said that yuh love me ma and I just wanted to kno if yuh really meant it or yuh was just sayin that because of how good I was fuccin yuh."* Reddot shot back, sitting up on the bed as well.

"Reddot, I meant it then n I still mean it now. I love yuh with all my heart babe; when I'm with yuh I feel complete. I never felt the way I feel about yuh for anybody else babe. Yuh really one of a kind n yuh treat me the way I'm supposed to be treated. So yes babe, I love yuh n I'm in love with yuh. There's nothing in this world that I wouldn't do for yuh because I kno that yuh would do the same for me." Shawny said, expressing her true feelings for Reddot.

"I aint even gone hole yuh babe." Reddot paused for a second trying to make sure that he didn't say the wrong thing. *"I'm not goin to sit here n act like I'm not in love with yuh as well, because I am ma. Yuh really mean a lot to me n I would really love to see where things would go between the two of us."* Reddot continued. *"But not to change the subject, I really need for yuh to do me a big favor."* he added, thinking of the perfect plan.

"Like I said babe, anythin for yuh my love n I do mean anythin." Shawny stated looking at Reddot directly in his eyes to let him know how much she really meant what

she said. Seeing the sincerity in Shawny's eyes, he knew right then and there that he had a keeper. Not trying to waste any more time, Reddot got down to all the demographics of his plans; letting Shawny know everything that she needed to do to make sure that everything went as planned.

Chapter Forty-Nine

There was nothing that Lil Rico hated more than the going back and forth to court; especially since he already knew that he wasn't going home. He was being charged with possession of a weapon on top of his parole violation. Lil Rico was also being held on a $100,000 bail, but being that he had a parole hold, he wasn't able to make bail even if he wanted to.

Lil Rico had been back from court already going to two hours, but he was still in the C95 intake waiting to get searched and sent back to his unit on the dark side. The dark side was where all the Crips were housed at. The C95 intake was one of the dirtiest intake on Riker's Island. The bull pen was always crowded with dope sick fiends being that it was the only building that provided methadone to the dope sick inmates.

"Yo my man can yuh slide over?" Lil Rico said to the fiend that had just taken a seat right next to where he was standing. The smell of shit sipped through his clothes. Not trying to get into any confrontation, the fiend did as he was asked and moved over.

The cold went off and all the C-Os in the intake area ran off to get in their riot gears. Twenty minutes later the same C-Os came through the intake's doors escorting four inmates in cuffs into the first holding pen. Since they were all placed in the same pen, it wasn't hard to figure out that they were all part of the same gang. After they were decontaminated, they were let out of pen #4 and placed into pen #5 same pen that Lil Rico was in.

"Ayo Domo!!! Ayo Dooommoo!!!" Lil Rico heard someone yell from the other pen across from him. *"Eeeeewaakkk!!! Wats popin! Wats popppppinnnn!!!"* Domo shouted out of the bullpen. *"Ayo scrap, wat happen, who y'all niggas got into it with?"*

"Wats poppin scrap! Niggas balled out on them hardbacks on the visit floor scrap!" Domo responded, not paying attention to his surroundings. *"Oh word!? Copy, say no more! Fuck them niggas scrap!"*

"Yuh kno the fuckin vibes!!!" Domo shot back. Lil Rico stood off to the side as he heard the disrespect. Lil Rico couldn't believe how dumb the Domo nigga was. He didn't bother to make sure that there wasn't any Crips in the bullpen before he started all the disrespect or he just didn't give a fuck.

Whether he knew the Crips or not, Lil Rico wasn't going to let the disrespect slide; not on his watch. Walking over to the corner, Lil Rico reached inside of his boxer briefs for his number 21 scalpel; after popping the plastic off he started to make his way over to where Domo and the other three bloods were standing and talking through the gates.

When he was within arm's reach, Lil Rico extended his hands, grabbed Domo by his shirt, pulled him towards himself and with his other hand he slapped the scalpel across the left side of Domo's face. Before Domo knew what was going on, he had a cut from one side of his face to the other.

Lil Rico backed off, putting enough room between him and Domo. Once they saw their homie holding his face, the other three bloods turned around, but not before Lil Rico was able to catch his second victim; giving him a cut on the back of his head that was sure to need a hundred and fifty stitches.

The other two bloods wasted no time jumping on Lil Rico. They were raining blows on Lil Rico nonstop. While they were putting the beat down of a life time on Lil Rico, all Lil Rico was worrying about was getting rid of the scalpel.

No weapon no case. The beating seem like it was ten minutes long but in reality it was only a few seconds. Before they knew it, all the intake C-Os had stormed into bullpen #5 to defuse the situation. When it was all said and done, Lil Rico and the four bloods were escorted out of the bullpen in handcuffs and on their way to the infirmary.

Chapter Fifty

It's been three days since True Blue went to Court and got remanded back into state custody to serve the last twelve months of his 2 to 4 years sentence. Leaving his family behind was one of the hardest things he ever had to do. He couldn't stop thinking about his lil' man – Ivan; he missed everything about him and wished like hell that he was still at home with him.

After being remanded into state custody, True Blue went out of his way to make sure that he was taken to the 5 building 'C95' on Rikers Island; same building and unit where Lil Rico and a few of his homies were housed at. Tired of playing Casino and sitting in the day room True Blue decided to give his family a call to see how they were holding up.

"This call is being recorded and monitored." the operator said before putting the call through. *"Hey babe! How yuh n the lil ones doin?"* True Blue said into the receiver once the call was connected.

"Hey my love! The kids are fine, the baby is takin a nap and Hailey is right here on her phone. As for me, I miss yuh so much babe, shit is not even funny. The house don't feel the same without yuh there; to the point that I rather just spend the night at my mother's house because bein at home reminds me so much of yuh." Aisha said, expressing the way she's been feeling since the day that True Blue had to turn himself in.

"Yeah I kno babe, I can only imagine how yuh feelin right now because I'm feelin the same way. Being away from yuh guys these past three days have been fuccin wit me ..." True Blue paused for a second before he continued. *"Listen babe, I kno that things aren't the way we had expected them to be. I kno that things are hard for the both of us at the moment, but I need yuh to try to hold it together my love; I need yuh to be strong n help me help yuh get through these hard times. I wont be in here for long and before we kno it, I'll be bacc home wit yuh guys like i never left."*

"I kno wat yuh sayin babe, but that dont change the fact that yuh would be gone for whole year babe. The baby is startin to look like yuh more n more as the days go by, lookin at him reminds me of yuh n when I think about yuh, reality hits me n knowin that yuh wont be with us for almost a year really breaks my heart babe." Aisha replied in almost a whisper.

True Blue knew that Aisha was hurting from the way she was speaking and that fact alone was breaking his heart into tiny pieces. The last thing he wanted to do was hurt his queen, his best friend and his better half.

"Everythin is goin to be fine babe, we just cant let this minor set bacc tear us apart my love." True Blue finally said after getting himself together. *"I kno babe, I kno; but anyways the baby is good, he's been a good boy these past three days. He's been lettin me sleep at night n all that."* Aisha stated changing the subject.

256

"Oh yeah? That's watssup! Make sure yuh tell him n my lil' Hailey that I called n asked for them; n that I said I love them n miss them with all my heart." True Blue shot back. *"I'll be more than happy to let the baby kno that his daddy called n asked for him the moment he wakes up. Hailey said that she loves yuh n miss yuh just as much as yuh miss her."*

True Blue and Aisha stayed on the phone for the remainder of the 15 minutes call; when the call hit 14 minutes, the phone beeped indicating that the call was coming to an end. *"Babe, this phone is about to hang up, I love yuh n the kids with all my heart! Take it easy out there for me. Don't stress ya'self to much babe, this would be over in no time."* True Blue said.

"Okay babe, I promise to try to take it easy n one step at a time my love. Before yuh called, I was online lookin to see when yuh have visits n it said that yuh have a visit on friday. So kno that me n the klids would be up there to see yuh my sexy hunny bunny! I love yuh Andy please be safe in there, stay out of trouble and tell Lil Rico that me n the kids said hi." Aisha stated before the call finally came to an end.

True Blue looked at the phone in disbelieve as he placed the receiver back on its hook. He missed his family dearly and he couldn't wait till the day that he would be finally back home with them.

Right there and then, True Blue made a promise to himself to never put his family through all the hurt that he was putting them through by being taken away from them. That was a promise that he planned on standing on no matter what it took; from that point on, his family happiness was going to be his main priority.

Chapter Fifty-One

"Damn Shawny wat the fuck yuh tryin to do to a nigga?"
Noni asked as he watched Shawny squat between his legs, take his dick out of his pant and put it in her mouth and started sucking on it nice and slow just like Noni liked it.

"I'm givin yuh somethin that I kno for a fact Asia dont do for yuh; or does she make love to ya dick the way i do?" Shawny stated as she guided Noni's dick in and out of her mouth, spitting on it and sucking it back up; making Noni's toes curl inside of his sneakers.

Noni and Shawny had been fucking behind Asia's back going on two months now. It all started one day when Shawny came out of the bathroom without a towel dripping wet and walked into the room that her sister and Noni shared.

"Shawn, wat the fuck?" Noni asked surprised, but in reality, he loved the view of Shawny's perfectly shaped body. Her camel toe was on full display and her nipples were nice and hard from the cold breeze of the room's AC hitting them.

"Oh shit, I'm sorry nigga! I aint kno yuh was in here." Shawny said. "I forgot to get my towel out of here yesterday when we did laundry. Shit! From the way yuh lookin, I kno that yuh love wat yuh see. Too bad that yuh cant handle all of this!" Shawny added, passing her left hand through her pussy.

Seeing this made Noni sit up on the bed while his dick grew in his pants. Noni always had a secret crush on

259

Shawny and often wished that one day she would let him fuck her brains out. *"Yeah, just like I thought! All talk no bite!"* Shawny said before she grabbed her towel and walked back out of the room swinging her ass from side to side and giving Noni a view that he would never forget.

Without wasting any time, Noni jumped off of the bed and followed Shawny back in to the bathroom. When he entered the bathroom, Noni pinned Shawny onto the bathroom sink. *"If yuh want me to fuck this pussy; all yuh have to do is say it ma, we to grown for the lil' ridles."* Noni said as he pressed his hand against Shawny's pussy. Shawny instantly became wet from Noni's touch.

"Does that answer ya question? Why dont yuh stop playin already n tear this pussy up nigga; or yuh just gon talk me to death?" Shawny shot back, with sarcasm all in her voice. Tired of Shawny's smart ass mouth, Noni turned her around and bend her over the bathroom sink, without a warning he entered her from the back and started fucking her fast and rough just like she liked it.

Ever since that day, Noni and Shawny had been fucking each other dry every time they were left alone in their apartment. *"Mmhhmmm, cum in my mouth daddy?"* Shawny begged, snapping Noni out of his train of thoughts. Not being able to hold back any longer, Noni gave Shawny what she had been asking for.

"Aaaaggghhhhh!!!" Noni moaned and came all in Shawny's mouth. Shawny made sure that she caught every

drop without letting anything hit the floor while she looked at Noni directly in his eyes making him weak at the knees.

After making sure that she had gotten every single drop of cum out of Noni's dick; Shawny got up from her squatting position, licked the corner of her lips, turned around and started to make her way in the direction of her room.

Ten minutes later Asia walked through the front door. Luckily Noni had already zipped up his pants and was now smoking on a blunt of grand daddy kush while watching the Boston Celtics vs. The Knicks game on ABC.

Chapter Fifty-Two

– Downstate Correctional Facility –

"Babe, tell me how I just got bacc from seein my counselor n the bitch talkin about I have to do two years n a half instead of the twelve months my lawyer said I was goin to be doin." True Blue said into the receiver once the call was put through. A week prior, True Blue was transferred to Down State Correctional Facility in Fishkill New York.

"Two years? Babe I thought yuh said yuh only had to do another twelve months? How the hell did the shit go up to another year n a half?" Aisha asked confused and frustrated.

"Babe, it's supposed to be twelve months babe, yuh was right there when the judge had credited me the twenty seven months that I had did before I was bailed out. For some reason they aint countin those twenty seven months n that's why I called yuh babe so that yuh can get my lawyer on the phone, to get him to fix this misunderstandin babe." True Blue stated.

"Smh, hold on babe, give me a second." Aisha replied. Within a few seconds Aisha had gotten True Blue's lawyer on the phone. *"Babe talk, he's on the line."* Aisha stated. *"Poul, wats the word? How yuh doin? Sorry for interruptin yuh but I needed to call yuh because I just came from seein my counselor n the lady talkin about that they aint credit me the time that I already had served prior to gettin bailed out."* True Blue said getting straight to the point.

"That's impossible Acosta; the judge said on records that yuh was bein credited for all the time you had already served. It has to be a misunderstandin n if that's the case, then give me a few days I'll have you back in front of the judge to get this situation fixed. Don't worry yourself, I got you." Poul responded, putting True Blue's and Aisha's mind at ease for the time being.

"Yes please Poul, I need yuh to take care of that for me ASAP! These people playin with my freedom n I'm not likin the shit not one bit." True Blue shot back. *"Like I said, it has to be a misunderstandin Acosta, just hold tight I'm goin to take care of it."* Poul said once again. *"Okay thank yuh Poul, hope yuh contine to have a great day today."* True Blue stated. *"Likewise!"* Poul shot back before ending the call.

True Blue and Aisha stayed on the phone for the remaining minutes. After speaking to Aisha and his kids, True Blue placed the phone receiver back on the hook and started to make his way back to his cell. *"I fuccin hate this Downstate shit."* True Blue said to himself as he walked into his assigned cell.

Downstate correctional facility was scored as a maximum correctional facility and it was a 23 and 1; inmates there were locked in for twenty three hours and only allowed to come out to get an hour of recreation. Downstate was a hold over jail and it would be the place wherein True Blue would be housed at, until he was designated and taken to his actual jail where he would be serving the remainder of his 2 to 4 years sentence.

Chapter Fifty-Three
– FBI HEADQUARTERS, NY. –

"The day we all have been waiting for has finally arrived! As of tomorrow, the streets of the Bronx would be a much better place. Tomorrow August 9th, 2017 would be the day when we put an end to the Hughes Avenue crew. Tomorrow, the streets of the south Bronx would be rid of these low life drug dealers and firearm traffickers." the chief of the FBI stated as every agent in attendance paid close attention to every word that came out of his mouth.

"These gangbangers would no longer be able to continue to infect our streets with their illegal doings. To our luck, Acosta, Valdez, Rodriguez and Richardson are already in State custody. Today I would be putting out a warrant for their arrest; tomorrow morning the US Marshall would have all three of these individuals in federal custody; there are still four individuals roaming the streets of the Bronx and our job is to make sure that they are off the street tomorrow before noon time. Let's not forget that our safety is our main priority, we are not to take any of these individuals lightly. I advise you all to get a much rest as you may need before tomorrow comes because it's going to be a very long day for us all. With that being said, thank you all for your time; see you all tomorrow morning at 6.00 Am." the chief of the FBI said in conclusion before stepping down from the podium and exiting out of the conference room.

A few minutes after the chief of the FBI had exited the conference room; all the agents in attendance exited the room as well, all lost in their own thoughts, mentally preparing themselves for the long day that they had ahead of them the next day.

Chapter Fifty-Four

"Ayo fatboii, bring ya ass down stairs with that bread nigga, I got shit to do!" Reddot said into the receiver as soon as he heard Cavs' voice on the other end of the phone. *"Fuck yuh nigga, I'll be there when I get there!"* Cavs shot back ending the call.

A few minutes later Cavs came strolling out of the building with his tail not too far behind C-Lite. Walking over to where Reddot was parked, Cavs opened the passenger door and jumped in. C-Lite opened the back door but was stopped by Reddot before he was able to enter the car.

"Yo Lite, give me and fatboii a minute let me holla at him real quicc cuhz." Reddot said. *"Oh okay, copy! Say no more loco."* C-Lite retorted shutting the cars door. *"Here nigga, this wat yuh came for right? It's all there."* Cavs said, handing Reddot a brown paper bag.

"Yuh sure is all there or do I have to count it?" Reddot asked looking inside of the bag. Cavs money was always on point but Reddot always like to rough up his feathers. *"Nigga yuh can count it if yuh want, but yuh would be wastin ya time. All $40,000 is in that bag nigga."* Cavs shot back. Reddot looked at Cavs for a few seconds before he reached over and grabbed the half of blunt that rested in the ash trey and lit it.

"Nigga yuh said yuh needed to holla at me, so start talkin bcos a nigga got shit to do too." Cavs said gettin tired of Reddot's little games. Reddot inhaled and exhaled the

267

smoke before he said *"I could be wrong but if I'm right then yuh gon be assed out. somethin is tellin me that yuh was the one behind Capo's murda nigga."*

"Wat the fuck yuh talkin about nigga! Yuh got me fucked up, Capo was my nigga I aint have no reason to kill him like that nigga!" Cavs shot back defsesively. Reddot was looking to get the smallest reaction from Cavs and without him knowin Cavs was showing him exactly what he wanted to see.

"It's cool, just kno that I'm doin my homework n if n when I find out that yuh was in fact behind my man gettin killed, I'm gon make yuh wish that yuh never crossed that line nigga." Reddot threaten. *"Nigga miss me with all the threats, like I said, I aint have no beef with Capo."* Cavs repeated.

"I kno yuh aint have nay issues with Capo, but maybe yuh thought that it was me behind those tints. Shit it was my car after all." Reddot stated, turning sideways to face Cavs. From the look on Cavs' face, he could tell that his last statement had changed Cavs' mood. Reddot wasn't a dummy and he picked up on the funny vibes immitiately.

"Nigga, miss me with the bullshit; I hope yuh done because I aint sittin here listenin to this bullshit yuh talkin." Cavs said. Reaching under his seat, he grabbed the blue Channel duffle bag and hopped out of the car, slamming the door behind him.

Reddot looked through the rear view mirror as Cavs and C-Lite made their way back into the buiding they had come out off. *"Dont worry fatboii, I got something special for yuh. Yuh can't fool me nigga."* Reddot thought to himself; putting the car in gear, Reddot pulled off from the front of the building.

Chapter Fifty-Five

– Marcy Correctional Facility –

The bus pulled into the Marcy Correctional Facility parking lot at around 3:30pm. In the bus, there were a total of 27 inmates with J-Rocc being one of those 27 inmates. *"I wont be stayin here too long."* J-Rocc kept telling himself as the bus came to a stop.

J-rocc was a Crip and in Marcy Correctional Facility, like 80% of the state jails, Marcy was one of the jails that Crip members weren't allowed to live in. J-Rocc knew this and of that fact alone, he planed on making sure he got out of there the first chance he got.

"Okay listen up! I dont kno wat jail yuh guys comin from, but in this facility we have Zero tolorence for the bullshit." The red neck C-O stepped into the bus and said. *"If n when I call y'all name, get up and get the hell off the bus. Richardson, Lopez, Bullock, Jones, Edward, Esprada and Linden. If I called ya name start makin ya way of this bus."* the red neck C-O said before steppin back off the bus.

A few seconds later all the inmates whose names had just been called made their way out of the bus. Every inmate was in shackle from the waist down to their feets making it almost impossible for them to walk let alone climb off the bus.

Once out of the bus, they were escorted into the intake area of the Marcy facility. As soon as the last inmate entered the intake area, the intake C-Os started to remove the shackles off of every inmate.

"Excuse me C-O can I please use the bathroom?" J-Rocc asked once he shackles were off. *"Yeah, go ahead but make it fuckin quick; I aint tryin to have all ya here crowdin my damn space!"* one of the other red neck C-Os responded.

Without saying a word J-Rocc got up from his seat and started to make his way in the direction of the bathroom. When he entered the bathroom, J-Rocc released his bladder, got in a squating position and push out the #15 scalpel out of hit rectum.

After wiping himself clean, he walked over to the sink to wash the scalpel and his hands. Popping the plastic, he walked back out of the bathroom and back into the intake area where the other inmates were.

J-Rocc walked over to one of the inmates that he knew as a blood, once he was within arms reach, J-Rocc swung the hand in which he held the scalpel and slapped it across the blood's face swiping it from one side of his face to the other; giving the blood a long clean cut from the left side of his face to the right side.

The hit was so smooth that it took the intake C-Os a few seconds to figure out what was going. *"Oh shit! Yuh cut me!"* the blood dude shouted catching everyone's attention. Instead of trying to fight J-Rocc off, the blood dude ran in the direction where all the intake C-Os were standing making it hot.

Whitin seconds J-Rocc was rushed by all ten of the intake C-O's and tackel to the floor. *"Didnt I fuckin tell yuh before gettin off that fuckin bus that we aint tolorating bullshit!"* one of the red neck C-Os was yelling as he and his coworkers beat the shit out of J-Rocc for the stunt he had just pulled.

When it was all said and done, J-Rocc was escorted to the S.H.U. while the blood dude was escorted to the infirmary to get his fresh cut taken care off. *"Fucc it, rather him than me."* J-Rocc thought to himself as he was escorted to the S.H.U.

Chapter Fifty-Six

"Ayo tribu, wat the fuck that nigga needed to holla at yuh about?" C-Lite asked Cavs once they stepped inside of the elevator. *"The nigga talkin about that he doin his homework on Capo's murda. He said that for some reason he thinks I was the one behind the hit."* Cavs said, a little too nonchalantly for C-Lite's liking.

"Wat? Nigga yuh sittin here actin like wat he said dont mean shit to yuh! I told yuh that this shit was goin to come back n bite us in the ass nigga but like always yuh thought yuh had everythin figured out n yuh fuckin didnt nigga." C-Lite shot back.

C-Lite has seen first hand how Reddot got down and he didn't want any part of that. Right there and then, C-Lite planned on doing whatever it took to make sure that he was in the clear.

"Nigga, calm ya scary ass down! The nigga dont kno shit, he's just fishin n tryin to see wat was my response goin to be; and if he does find out, fuck it! Wat the fuck we gon be able to do other than to bring the heat to tha nigga! Yuh act like the nigga is untouchable. I missed him once, but I promise yuh I won't miss him again if n when he comes over here on some bullshit!" Cavs retorted, meaning every word spoken.

The truth of the matter was that Cavs didn't care if Reddot knew or not that he was the one behind Capo's

273

murder. Cavs was tired of Reddot and by his action, it was very clear that he was.

Once the elevator reach their floor, without sayin another word Cavs and C-Lite exited the elevator and made their way back into their apartment. *"I wish that nigga would come back over here on some bullshit. I got something special waitin for his ass."* Cavs thought to himself.

Chapter Fifty-Seven

Boo woke up at around 8.00am and for some reason something felt off. His gut feeling was tellin him that something was off; he just couldn't figure out what it could be. Being that Star and their son had a doctor's appointment, Boo was the only one left in the apartment. Before rolling out of bed, Boo reached under his pillow for his F&N; after making sure that it was off safety, he tucked it in his lower back.

'BOOM! BOOM!!' Hearing the front door of his apartment being kicked open, Boo panicked and pulled out his F&N and pointed it toward the bedroom's door. Within seconds, the room's door was also kicked open.

"FBI! Step out the room with your hands in the air! We know that you are in there!" Boo heard a voice say from outside of the room. *"Wat the fucc is goin on?"* Boo thought to himself confused.

"I'm not going to repeat myself! Come out of the room with your hands where we can see them!" Not trying to get shot and killed in the process, Boo laid his F&N on his bed and started to make his way out of the room's door with his hands in the air.

As soon as he stepped one foot outside of the room, he was rushed by five federal agents, all wearing flight jackets with the 'FBI' letters written across the front of it in bold yellow letters.

- - -

– Meanwhile ... –

"Oohhh! Yessss daddy, fuck this pussy! Yes! Fuck this pussy like is ya last time fuckin it babbbbyyy." Shantel, Remo's baby-mother moaned. *"Yuh love this dicc baby? Tell me yuh love this dicc ma."* Remo responded as he continued to fuck Shantel in the doggy style position. Sweat was dripping off his forehead onto Shantel's lower back.

"Yes! I-I-lo-loooo-vveee this dick baby!!!" Shantel moaned. *"Put a finger in my butt babe! Please put a finger in my buttttttt!!!"* she added in between moans. Right when Remo was about to do just as Shantel was asking, the door to their bedroom was kicked open.

"FBI! Don't fucking move! Put your hands where I can see them!" Remo heard someone behind him yell. Pulling out of his baby-mother's pussy, Remo tried to jump off the bed and reach for the gun that laid on the night stand right next to the bed.

"GUNNNN!!!" one of the agents shouted and within seconds they was all on top of Remo like white on rice, before he was able to get a hold on his gun. By now Shantel was being escorted out of the room by a female agent with no clothes on, still drenched in sweat and with her wetness dripping down the side of her legs.

"Wat the fucc y'all niggas want! I aint do shit! Let me the fucc go!" Remo was saying, trying to fight the agents off,

276

but to no avail. Remo was in a fact a strong individual, but he was not strong enough to fight off all eight of the FBI agents.

"*Daddddyyyy !!!*" Remo's kids shouted as he was being led out of their apartment in handcuffs.

- - -

– UP THE BLOCK –

"*Ayo ock, let me get a pack of Newport n a three dollar pack of fronto.*" Montana said to the ock that was behind the counter. "*That's $12.75*" the ock behind the counter retorted placing Montana's items into a black bag.

Montana reached in his pockets and handed the ock a $20 bill. After getting his change, Montana grabbed his merchandize and started to make his way out of the store, but before he was completely out of the store three white guys in all black suits ruched him onto the floor.

"*Kevin 'Montana' Rivers, you are under arrest. Everything you say can and will be used against you in the Court of law. You have the right to remain silent*" After hearing the word "under arrest" Montana's world went blank.

Montana couldn't believe what was happening or why it was happening. All he knew was that he was being under arrest and from the way the three white guys were dressed, deep down inside he knew that they were the FEDs.

Chapter Fifty-Eight

– What Goes Around Comes Around –

"Shawny, not for nothing, but yuh dead need to stop shakin ya ass for money; yuh fuckin with me now so there's no need for yuh to be doin that shit anymore" Noni said. *"Yuh kno im goin to take care of yuh ma."* he added. Ever since Asia started working overnight as a Registered Nurse in Lincoln Hospital, Noni and Shawny was able to spend more time with one another.

The two even had sex in the same bed that Noni shared with her sister. The power of the pussy was a motherfucker and Shawny knew that; that's why she used what God had given her to her full advantage. She had him wrapped around her hands her and she wouldn't want it any other way.

"Yeah I get wat yuh sayin pa' n trust me I'm just doin this for the time bein until I figure somethin out. I kno that yuh would take care of me, but I'm a boss bitch n I like to take care of myself. I never been the type to let a nigga take care me. I can do that on my own pa'." Shawny replied while sitting up on the bed and giving Noni a kiss on his lips.

"Listen babe, today I would be gettin out of work at 3.00 am, do yuh think yuh would be able to come pick me up? I have somethin real especial that I want to show yuh." Shawny added squeezing Noni's dick through his sweat pants.

"Come on ma, yuh kno I would do that for yuh n more. All yuh have to do is ask." Noni retorted grabbing a handful of Shawny's ass. *"Just hit my line 15 minutes before yuh get off so that I can head out."* he added.

"Okay daddy, I will do. Let me get out this bed before I be late for work." Shawny said rolling out of her sister's bed. Noni watched Shawny's ass swing from side to side until she finally out of his eye sight.

- - -

– Starletts Gentlemen's Club –

For the past five hours, Shawny had been shaking her ass nonstop; it got to the point where her feet was hurting from all the walking that she been doing for the past five hours in her 6 inch heels. Five hours later and she was $2,500 richer.

Shawny was ready to call it a night. Walking into the dressing room, Shawny walked over to her locker and opened it. Taking out her cell phone, she sent Noni a text. A few seconds later, a text from Noni came through. *'Copy ma, I'm on my way. Be there in 25minutes.'* Noni's text read. Reading the text once more, Shawny smiled to herself as she placed her phone back into her Channel bag.

Just as promised, twenty five minutes later, Noni walked into the club like he owned the place; spotting Shawny talking to a few of her coworkers by the bar, Noni made his way over to them. *"Watssup sexy! Yuh ready to go?"* Noni asked once he was close enough for Shawny to hear him over the loud music.

"Oh, hey yuh! I didn't even see yuh walk in." Shawny turned around and said, embracing Noni into a hug and grabbing his dick in the process. *"Yes I'm ready to go pa'."* Shawny whispered in Noni's ears.

Not trying to waste any more time, the two love birds headed for the exit of the club holding hands. When they got outside of the club, Shawny and Noni made their way in the direction where Noni's G-wagon was parked at, ignorant to the fact that they were being closely watched by a second pair of eyes.

Getting in the truck, Noni pushed the start botton bringing the foreign spaceship to life. Right when he was about to put the truck in gear, he felt a cold metal on the back of his head. *"Oh my gawd!"* Shawny screamed scared as she saw the biggest gun she has ever seen pressed to the back of the head of her lover.

"Don't even think about it nigga." the voice behind the mask said; stopping Noni from reaching for the gun that lie under his seat. *"Keep that noise down ma, before i make yuh myself."*. The gun man added, mean mugging Shawny through his ski mask.

"Come on man wats this about? I got money if that wat yuh want. All yuh gotta do is take me to it n its' yours playa." Noni said shaking in his pants. *"Nah nigga, Yuh got me fucked up, I want more than just money nigga."* the voice

280

behind the mask shot back while removing the mask off his face. Looking through the rear view mirror Noni made eye contact with one of his worst enemies.

"*Oh shit! Reddot! Wat yuh want from me now? I left the X just so that y'all can continue to eat without havin to worry about me n my nigga.*" Noni pleaded. "*I got $250,000 in the crib that yuh can have.*" he added. There was nothing in the world that Reddot hated the most beside a bitch nigga, a nigga that did as he pleased in the streets but when the tables turned he pleaded and begged for his life.

"*Babe ya work here is done, do me a favor n take my car bacc to the crib, I'll meet yuh there once I get done with this fucc nigga.*" Reddot said. Without a second thought, Shawny did as she was told. The look on Noni's face was priceless.

"*Wat nigga? Don't look like that yuh gettin wat yuh deserve fuck nigga!!*" Shawny said spitting directly in Noni's face before stepping out of the truck. If looks could kill; from the way Noni was looking at Shawny, she would have dropped dead right where she sat.

"*Come on Reddot I'll give yuh all the money I have; just let a nigga live. I'll even skip town; yuh won't have to worry about seein me ever again my nigga.*" Noni continued to plead for his life. "*Nah my nigga, yuh should have thought of that before yuh did my man Legend the way yuh did. Wat! Yuh thought yuh goin to get away wit that?*" Reddot shot back.

281

Tired of all the crying and begging that Noni was doing, Reddot crashed his .357 as hard as he could on the back of Noni's head, knocking him out cold. *"Yeah, yuh gon skip town alright, but after I get don with ya bitch ass!"* Reddot said to Noni's unconscious body.

To be continued...

Epilogue

SMACK! SMACK!! The sound of Reddot's .357 making contact with Noni's face was all that was heard all over the abandoned warehouse located in the Hunts Point Area of the Bronx.

Reddot had Noni bound to a chair, in his birthday suit. For that past three hours Reddot has been trying to get Noni to talk; but not even after being badly beating and losing the top front row of his teeth had Noni uttered a word: making Reddot hotter then what he already was.

"Nigga, yuh think this shit is a game?" Reddot asked, gripping Noni's badly beaten face, forcing him to look him in the eyes. *"This is the last time I'm goin to ask ya bitch ass. Who the fucc gave yuh the drop on my man Legend, nigga?"* Reddot asked once more.

The work that Reddot has been putting on Noni's for the past three hours had Noni almost unconscious. The swollen lips; coupled with the pain of his teeth being knocked out was making it almost impossible for Noni to talk even if he wanted to.

With the little bit of strength that Noni had left in his body, he gathered all the spit mixed with blood in his mouth and spat right on Reddot's face. *"Nigga, yuh better off killin me my nigga, because I aint tellin ya bitch ass shit!"* Noni finally said through his swollen lips. With the back of his left hand, Reddot wiped the spit off of his face, then looked at Noni and smiled at his brazenness.

Out Now!!!

Homicide Hatford By King Thomas

The Akbar Story 'A Brooklyn Tale' By King Thomas

The Stars Represent You & Me By Aswad Thomas

A Hustler's Fatal Attraction By King Thomas

Coming Soon!!!

H-Blocc Part 2 by A.Acosta

Ballers Ambition By King Thomas

Belly Of The Beast By King Thomas

A Gangsta Seduction Part 1 By King Thomas

A Gangsta Seduction Part 2 By KIng Thomas

The Akbar Story Part 2. By King Thomas

The Town By B-EZY

Philly Chaos By Lamar Sampson

Born In The Grave Part 1. By Self Made Tay

Born In The Grave Part 2. By Self Made Tay

County Of Kingz By Jay Quizzy

About the Author

My name is Ariel Acosta, I'm 28 years old and I'm 5'10, 170lbs.

I'm currently serving a 13 year sentence at U.S.P Canaan, for Conspiracy to distribute Crack Cocaine and Trafficking Firearms charges. My case is awaiting a decision in the Court of Appeal. If and when my appeal is granted, five years would be deducted off my sentence which means that my 13 year sentence would be reduces down to 8 years. I have been in Federal custody going on four years now, if my sentence is reduced to 8 years I would only have another two and a half years left to do.

Novels would not be the only way you would be hearing from me. I also write music and I'm also working on my clothing line called IVAN "I.V." ACOSTA CLOTHING & CO.

I would really appreciate it if you guys would take a ride with me on this journey; I promise that I won't let y'all down!

#TRUEBLUE

#TOP30HIMSELF...

Follow me on Instagram: *@TRUESHMURDAA* if you want to stay in tune with me and everything I have going on.

Made in the USA
Middletown, DE
09 August 2021